THE GIRL WITH MAGIC IN HER VOICE

THE GIRL WITH MAGIC IN HER VOICE

A rare story, tender and sweet

Dedicated to millions of country music fans

By
Douglas E. Bean

ISBN 0-9653609-0-3

This book is a work of fiction, but a salute to many well known country music stars who are mentioned with respect and admiration, plus dedication to the millions of country music fans.

Published by Douglas E. Bean
6709 Newman Street
Boise, Idaho 83704

Printed by The Caxton Printers, Ltd.
312 Main Street
Caldwell, Idaho 83605

Dedicated to four fine sons—Doug, Steve, Dave, and Greg; to four fine daughters-in-law—Cindy, California Linda, Idaho Linda, and Tina; to five charming granddaughters—Christy, Heidi, Clare, Margaret, and Bethany; to a sturdy grandson—Charles; and to a rambunctious great grandson—Chance.

To Susan. Is she really alive?

And especially to the millions of
country music fans.

The author greets President Harry Truman at Sun Valley in 1949. Reference is made to this picture on page 38 of the book.

RARE PHOTOS—At top is picture of Charles Lindbergh, right, and then Major Joe Foss. Author took the picture on island of Emirau in western Pacific in June 1944. Major Foss was first American war ace in Pacific.

Right photo shows author with Major Foss, who was commander of a Marine Air Wing on Emirau Island.

At bottom, a short snorter dollar bill autographed by Charles Lindbergh and Major Joe Foss. This collector's item and the other two photos are described on page 37 of book.

The dollar bill may be the only one in existence, autographed by Lindbergh and Foss, indeed a valuable collector's item.

Contents

FOREWORD

If you are looking for violence, vulgarity, and trash sex, don't read this book. If you are one of the many millions who are disgusted with cheap movies, TV shows, and sleazy talk show hosts, you should enjoy this sweet and tender story. There's no trash, and the book is dedicated mainly to country music.

I wonder how many folks realize that country music is the only segment of the entertainment industry that does not offer vulgarity and violence, and tasteless themes.

Country music is clean, vigorous, enjoyable, and appealing, with a wide range of stars and wide range of different styles of music. That is why more and more people are turning from movies and TV and appreciating country music.

This story is about The Girl With Magic In Her Voice. I submit it is one of the sweetest and most tender books you will ever read.

You will recognize many of the names, because they are names of real people. I salute these people with respect and admiration for their many sparkling talents.

Since this is an entirely fictitious story, the other names mentioned are in no way real persons. They were invented strictly for purposes of telling the story.

There are two or three episodes where there might be a semi-naughty word or two, but no vulgarity. These scenes just put a little deviltry into the tell. There are a couple of sad scenes, which might bring a tear or two, but there are other amusing parts to offset the sadness and hopefully bring some chuckles.

There is no trashy sex, but a couple of innocent happenings between the narrator and the girl with magic in her voice, whose name is Susan.

There is a surprise ending, and this story is meant to be enjoyed and memorable.

Douglas E. Bean
Boise, Idaho
January 1996

THE GIRL WITH MAGIC IN HER VOICE

The late model sedan turned through the cemetery gates, wound around several curves, and stopped beneath a towering evergreen tree. The figure of a tall, white-haired man slowly climbed out of the car, something in hand, and walked across the grass to a white marble tombstone. He knelt and placed a fresh crimson rose by the stone which was inscribed: "Susan Sanders, 1974–1995, Magic in Her Voice."

The sad smile on his face did not come close to reflecting the deep hurt in his heart.

* * * * *

This story is a little about me, the tall man, but mostly about Susan Sanders, a truly beautiful young black girl. It is about how trust and love slowly developed between these two so entirely different people, how they found a deep happiness, not in romance, but in devotion to each other.

It is about a 50-year-old song, written by me, titled "Home in Tennessee," a song which had its beginnings in the south and west Pacific during World War II. It is about how I found the original arrangements of the song in an old suitcase full of junk only a couple of years ago, and how I at once started looking for a girl with magic in her voice to sing it.

As stated, the story is about Susan, who was nineteen years old when first we met. Susan resembled closely a younger Allison Payne, the comely WGN-TV anchor out of

Chicago. Susan was tall, slimly built, with long black locks, but healthfully developed in the right places.

It is about Susan, who at first held a deep dislike—almost a hatred—of all white men, including me.

Just a few words about me . . . born in Knoxville, grew up there and went to school there, but moved to Idaho over 50 years ago in 1942. Spent two and a half years in the Navy in World War II, moved from Pocatello to Twin Falls and then to Boise for the past 30 years. Yeah, I'm an old buzzard, had my fortieth birthday for the second time in 1995, and have learned that a thirty or forty minute beauty sleep at noon in a great refresher.

Susan at heart was a sparkling beauty, but it took time for a friendship to develop between her and the white man. Slowly and gradually, a fragile relation started, then blossomed into full trust and warm mutual affection. There was never any thought of romance, and never any hanky panky. They were not in love, but Susan would say later she loved the white man like a grandfather. This is a tender story of a young woman who was hit with polio at age seven, fought fiercely and masterfully to overcome a weak left leg, and rose to prominence in the entertainment world because of her unlimited, versatile talents topped off by the magic in her voice.

Since I'm telling the story, you'd better know my name. It is Douglas Bradford, for the record, and most people call me Doug. As I write, I am deeply worried whether I have the ability and the talent to tell an almost unbelievable story and make it believable, because this story is true.

A little background is necessary. The Navy grabbed me in the summer of 1943. I had been One-A from the start, but was married and the wife was expecting our first child in December.

A couple of days before going to Chattanooga to be sworn in, I made a special trip to Gatlinburg, and then up a dirt/gravel road to the foot of Mt. LeConte, which I had climbed several times in past years.

I drank in the beauty and majesty of those Smoky Mountains, breathing deeply of pure and clear air, good for one's soul, and very invigorating.

Six months later, I was in the south and west Pacific, in a Seabee stevedore battalion, a good example of another Navy snafu, since I knew nothing of loading and unloading ships.

The sameness of hot and humid weather, which tends to dull one's mind, the daily afternoon downpour of tropical rains, and the very dullness of existence made me long to be back close to the Smoky Mountains in East Tennessee. A tune started buzzing around in my head, reflecting the deep desire to get back to Knoxville and Gatlinburg and the mountains.

I was discharged in November 1945, got back to Knoxville, and had no trouble picking out the tune on Mother's piano. The family, of course, thought it was an extra nice tune. One night, after everybody else had gone to bed, I sat at the kitchen table and tried to fit some words and create a real song. I was amazed the next morning. The words fit, the words rhymed, and the song told a story—three ingredients a good song should have.

Tennessee, callin' me, to the land I love;
Riding hard, headin' home, where I'm dreamin' of;
Mountains glistenin' in the sun;
Purple hills when day is done;
Friendly folks to say hello;
Folks you love, and folks you know, till
Here at last, home again, home in Tennessee;
Stars above to guide the way;
Wearing ridin' night and day;
Long long trail before me lies;

But I'm gettin' near with each sunrise;
'Till here at last, home again, back home in
Tennessee.

PRETTY TUNE FOR THE WORDS

Those words on a piece of paper don't reflect very much, but there's a pretty tune to make them sound real appealing.

Moving to Twin Falls after the war, I realized that Idaho would fit the title just the same as Tennessee, so for a couple of years it became an Idaho song. The best band in town, directed by a popular guy named Arlen Bastion, played it for awhile at the Turf Club, Twin Falls' nicest, but no demand developed for it, so the original was stashed away in an old suitcase.

After moving to Boise in 1966, a series of events started unfolding. In the fall of 1993, I cleaned out the old suitcase and found a somewhat dog-eared copy of the Tennessee song. On my new Yamaha organ keyboard, I struggled to learn to play it, and progressed enough to hit only a few sour notes. I swear it was even prettier than I remembered. Again I started thinking of trying to find a girl with magic in her voice to sing it, but didn't come close.

In the winter I made an appointment with Dr. Jerry Schroeder, a likeable Boise State University music professor. A very friendly sort in a small office in the Performing Arts Center, dominated by a piano, his desk and a shelf of books, he looked at the Xerox copy of the song, sat at the piano, played it a couple of times, and these were his words, "My gosh, that's a pretty song." Then he made a recording on his little recorder. It was then that I asked him to help find a girl who could sing the song the way it should be sung. I wanted to find a young women with magic in her voice, but who was attractive with a sparkling personality. He was more than willing, but pointed out it would take time.

A month later, he called to say that he had four college girls who would like to audition the song in his office at eleven the next morning.

I was there, and the miracle started to develop, although it got off to a rocky start.

Only three girls were there at first, and all had nice voices. I think their names were Jean, Penny, and Clarine. Another young women came through the office door. I was standing at the piano, and the newcomer said she had heard the tune out in the hall, liked it, and asked for me to play it.

Dr. Schroeder explained that the new girl's name was Susan. She was a beautiful young black girl.

There was no smile on Susan's face as I stumbled through the playing. Again, she gave orders to me to scoot over on the piano bench, so she sat down and scooted me. I slid a little too far, and lit on my rump on the floor, laughing easily. The girls helped me up, and asked if I was hurt. I said no, I had landed on my brains, patting myself on the backside. The girls and professor smiled, and then I pointed to Susan and said rather directly, "Young women, you are the first girl in 50 years to knock me on my ass." Everybody howled but Susan, who kept only a stony face.

Then she started playing the song, and her voice was a pure thrill to hear. I sensed right then that here was the girl with magic. The professor and the other three girls realized that same thing. The professor said he had a meeting to go to, and the girls left with my hearty thanks for showing up.

The professor commented on his way out, "I'll leave you and Susan to get acquainted."

SUSAN THE ICEBERG

Susan took a seat in one of the chairs, looked at me, and said rather icily, "What are you going to say now, Mr. Bradford?"

I replied slowly, "All I want to say is that you have the most beautiful voice I have ever heard. I believe you could have a brilliant singing career, and I would like to help in any way I can. But, first you ought to stop acting like an iceberg and try to be just a little bit on the friendly side. Is that possible?"

She snapped back, "I don't feel friendly, so there is nothing to talk about, is there?"

"Very well," I returned in my own cool voice. "I'm glad to have met you and I say again you have something special—almost a magic in your voice and you should take advantage of it. Hope to see you later."

She actually glared at me, and then said unhappily, "I hate to ask favors, but I missed my ride home, so would you drop me off somewhere so I can get a cab?"

I asked where she lived, and she said West Boise, which is where I live, so I told her to come on, I'll take her home. She hesitated, but finally replied stonily, "Okay."

Walking to my car, I noticed for the first time she was limping in her left leg.

"So you noticed," she said bitterly. "Yeah, I've got a bum leg and it's none of your business."

I opened the car door for her, started to help her in, but she brushed me aside angrily and climbed in by herself.

I ventured quite delicately, "It's noon time, and my belly is growling. Could you stand a bit to eat?"

"Just take me home," she answered icily.

Susan directed me to a nice residential street in West Boise, and we pulled up to the front of an attractive two-story house.

"If you'll sit still, I'll come around and help you out," I offered.

Susan said an emphatic "No" and got out herself and started to the front door. Just then, an extra attractive black woman came out of the door, saw us and said, "Please come in." Susan was doing her best to shake her head vigorously at her mother's invitation and to quit being so nice, but acting on impulse, I followed Susan into the front room.

I introduced myself, and the lady said she was Gloria, Susan's mother. It was easy to see where Susan got her own beauty.

The living room was comfortable, and Mrs. Sanders waved me to a chair. Susan was scowling, but also sat down.

Mrs. Sanders asked, "Are you a friend of Susan's?"

I replied, "No, we are not friends, but about an hour ago I heard your daughter sing a song I had written and she had the most beautiful voice I had ever heard," adding that I suggested to Susan she should give some serious thought to a singing career.

Susan interrupted angrily. "How could I ever do that with this bum leg?"

"Susan," I answered evenly, "would you at least listen to an idea I have? I'm thinking big, and all I'm asking is that you make a tape of that song and I will try to get some important people to listen to it."

Susan sniffed, totally unimpressed. She responded coolly, "Just who do you think is important who would listen?"

I replied calmly, "I would aim for Crook and Chase on the Music City Tonight show on TNN. Would that be important enough?"

Mrs. Sanders broke in with excitement. "Oh, we watch Lorianne and Charlie almost every night. Susan's father Eric and I are pretty good country music fans." Susan was almost derisive, with her doubt in plain sight.

I said rather coldly to Susan, "If you can get off your high horse tomorrow and make that recording, you won't have to be so snotty anymore. If you get out of school at 2:30, as you said, let me pick you up in front of the Performing Arts Building, and I'll make a date with a studio in Garden City. Okay?"

"It will be a waste of time, but I'll be there." Susan said as coldly as before.

I left, torn between the richness of her voice and her angry attitude.

It was almost astounding, but Susan was there the next afternoon right on time. She climbed into the car, saying nothing.

Then, on the way to the recording studio which I had reserved, she offered this, quite surprisingly, "When I sing, I'm not mean and ornery, because music is sort of a refuge and helps me forget other troubles."

We got to the appointment on time, Susan sitting at the piano and practicing a few notes. I had told her I hoped she would put her heart into the song.

She turned to the operator and said "Let it roll." The operator, unbarbered and rather hippie looking, smiled and hit a button.

Susan could have charmed everybody in town, the pure, rich way she delivered. Little chills ran up and down my spine, and the operator listened with his mouth wide open.

When Susan finished, he blurted, "My God, Lady, that's the most wonderful singing I have ever heard." I agreed 10,000 percent, and saw that Susan's face and manner had softened.

I got four copies of the tape, we played the original, and it sounded pure and rich, and then we left. The tapes cost forty-five dollars each.

Susan had a questioning look on her face and I explained, "One copy is for you and your family, one is for me, and the other two will go to Nashville with me in a few days. I hope you will start dreaming big with me."

"What will happen in Nashville?" Susan asked.

I merely replied, "If I can get Jim Owens, the producer, and Lorianne and Charlie, to listen to the tape, I believe there is a good chance you would be invited to Nashville for an audition for Music City Tonight."

Susan was unmoved. "How would I get there?" she asked bluntly.

My answer: "I would go along, and invite your mother or father to go, too. If they can't get away, you and I would go."

Susan, in an angry voice, started to erupt, but I broke in and said rather sharply, "Susan, if we go together, you would have complete privacy in your room, and I would have the same in my room. You would not be insulted or hassled in any way and you would be as safe as if you were in your own home. I am old enough to be your grandfather, and I am interested only in getting you to agree to help a long-shot miracle happen so a lot of people in this country can hear your voice. If you don't believe that, we might as well forget the whole thing right now, but I hope you will decide that you have guts enough to at least try, if the opportunity is there. What do you say?"

Susan flared, "I've got guts enough, mister, and you better believe it. I've had guts all my life, and since you put it that way, I'll go and have a try at it. I just don't think there is any chance of getting anywhere."

She added caustically, "And now, what will you do next?"

I thought a moment, then said calmly, "I will make a call Monday morning, since tomorrow is Saturday, and try to persuade Jim Owens and staff just to listen to your tape. I'll bet you a thousand to one they will love it and invite you to come to Nashville for an audition." No problem in getting the phone number of Jim Owens, but his secretary, whose name was Elaine, said he was busy all day. Since I don't have much charm with women, I told Elaine that all I wanted was fifteen minutes with Mr. Owens and staff to hear the sensational voice of a young woman from Boise on tape. I stressed to Elaine that it would be one of the best investments Mr. Owens could make, only fifteen minutes of his time, with Lorianne and Charlie to be there, too. Elaine must have recognized the urgency in my voice, so she said she would confer with Jim Owens and call back. She sounded sincere and another part of the miracle unfolded. She said Mr. Owens had agreed to give me fifteen minutes, and if the following Monday was convenient, for me to be there with the tape.

I called Susan later in the week and told her that her tape had a date in Nashville with the producer and stars of Music City Tonight. I suggested lunch at the University cafeteria and that is where we ate with not much conversation. Other students were curious but paid little attention to a white-haired white man and a young black girl.

When she went back to a class, I smiled broadly that lunch was nice, that I enjoyed being with her, and would call when I got back from Nashville. All she said was short, "Okay, see you when you get back." I thought to myself, she could at least have said break a leg.

THE ROAD TO NASHVILLE

Sort of an empty feeling to take along, but I headed for Nashville the following Sunday morning leaving mountain time Boise a little after eight, nonstop United's friendly skies to central time Chicago a little after one. An hour layover, time to get a sandwich and have a couple of cigarettes, on to Nashville, arriving late in the afternoon.

An Opryland Hotel bus picked up passengers and I was safely in my room by six. This magnificent hotel is deeply impressive and I spent a couple of hours just strolling around marvelling at its beauty.

The next morning I cabbed to McGavock Street and had no trouble finding the offices of Jim Owens and Associates. I went in, asked for Elaine, introduced myself, and thanked her sincerely for arranging this meeting. In a moment, she took me into the Owens office and he was meeting with Lorianne and Charlie planning for the night's show. Jim Owens was tall, with white/gray hair, quite distinguished looking, and this side of fifty. Lorianne was dressed casually in blouse and slacks, a far cry from her usual glowing appearances on Music City Tonight. Charlie had on a pair of Levis that had seen plenty of previous service. We all shook hands, and frankly, it was a big thrill for me just to be in the same room as these famous people.

Mr. Owens came right to the point. "Mr. Bradford," he commenced, "you asked for fifteen minutes for us to hear a young singer from Boise, Idaho. Elaine, who is really the boss around here, detected something in your voice that made her put you on my schedule. Let's hear your singer."

Jim placed the tape in the recorder, and they sat back with curious looks on their faces.

Then Susan's pure unforgettable voice came through, and there was just one word for the three listeners. It was "spellbound."

Susan's voice faded into silence and they seemed mesmerized. Without a word, Jim rewound the tape, and played it again.

Owens shook his head almost in disbelief. "That is one of the most remarkable voices I have ever heard." Lorianne and Charlie agreed wholeheartedly. I told them that there were no enhancements; that it was Susan's voice they heard in all its purity.

This was the time for the question. "Mr. Owens," I started, "I think Susan would be a great hit if you introduced her on Music City Tonight. May I bring her to Nashville for an audition?"

He didn't hesitate. "By all means, bring her as soon as convenient." Lorianne and Charlie echoed his decision.

Almost as an afterthought, Mr. Owens asked questions about Susan. I advised briefly, "Susan is a nineteen-year-old beautiful African-American girl, who limps slightly on her left leg because of polio which hit when she was seven years old. She has unlimited talent with her voice and the piano. She will graduate from Boise State University in a year and a half, and she has no bad habits with booze or drugs, and she is all business. All of you will love her."

My fifteen minutes had extended to an hour. It was decided that Susan should come to Nashville in three weeks, on a Monday like today. I left, with a feeling of jubilation, after asking Elaine to call and let us know the time and place.

I really didn't need a cab back to the hotel, feeling like soaring on Cloud Nine. I forgot to say that for breakfast I had ham and eggs and red eye gravy, some fried grits, and hot biscuits and honey, the delicious kind of food I missed out west.

I considered calling Susan immediately, but decided to wait until getting back to Boise. I found a place in Nashville, "Ye Olde Music Shoppe" and bought copies of several songs I remembered from the 30s and 40s.

I got back to Boise late the next afternoon, called Susan from the airport and asked if I could drop by in about forty-five minutes. She said very neutrally that it was okay.

I pulled up in front of her house and Gloria, her

mother, opened the door and invited me in. I went into the living room, and there were Eric, her father, and Sally, her younger sister.

I said formally, "Miss Sanders, you are invited to audition in Nashville in three weeks for an appearance on Music City Tonight."

For a moment her eyes lit up with excitement, but then she only commented, "So you pulled it off."

I corrected her rather gently. "Nope, it was your voice that pulled it off. Mr. Owens and Lorianne and Charlie all heard the tape twice, and that is why you are invited."

"There is only one question to be asked: Will you go to Nashville with just you and me? You will have to learn to trust me, and you have my word of honor you will not be troubled in any way. Young lady, I believe it will be a chance of a lifetime for you and very bright future for you. Will you go?"

Susan had an uncertain look on her face, then she sighed, "I reckon I'll have to trust you. Yeah, I'll go."

I replied honestly. "That's the greatest news I've heard in a long, long time. I'll say please, ma'am, will you start giving some thought to the possibility that we just might become good friends, with complete trust in each other? Right now, that is my main hope."

Susan gave a small smile, and just barely murmured, "We'll see." I grinned happily and merely commented, "It's a start. You can arrange to miss a couple of days at school on that Monday and Tuesday, and we can have lunch a couple of times."

"And young lady, I bet you a thousand to one your tape would get you the audition. Now I'll bet you ten thousand to one you will be invited to be on Music City Tonight. And another thing—at the moment you get the invitation, you are going to get the biggest hug that any man ever gave a woman."

Eric and Gloria had smiles on their faces; Sally was wide-eyed at what I had dared to say.

With that, I left.

NASHVILLE AHEAD

Time went by quick for me the next couple of weeks. Susan hadn't thawed out too much, but we had lunch about three times, and she was friendly, if quite reserved. We had a bite the Friday before the Sunday morning we would take off, so I told her to be ready at six forty-five and I would pick her up then, to pack only one suitcase plus her carry on bag. Jim Owens had said the audition would be casual and informal, so Susan brought only a couple of slack outfits.

The young woman was remarkable because she was waiting right on time Sunday morning, and her father Eric, mother Gloria, and sister Sally were all up, too.

Eric said it best. "Mr. Bradford, all the family—and I believe that includes Susan—trusts you. Take good care of our daughter, and we will be waiting to hear how she does."

"Mr. Sanders," I assured him, "Susan is a cinch to be a big hit and she will be invited to be on Music City Tonight, and we will call you right after the audition."

We waved goodbye and got to the airport with plenty of time to spare. Susan had had a piece of toast and glass of milk so she wasn't hungry yet.

The friendly skies got us to Chicago in good shape. An hour layover provided time for a couple of cigarettes, and I thought I detected Susan frowning a bit when I lit up. We arrived in Nashville late afternoon.

In the Opryland limousine, which picks up guests at the airport, Susan gave a small smile and asked if I had noticed that she was a little nervous. I hadn't noticed and said so.

"Well," she stated, "this was my first ride in an airplane, and I'm glad the pilot drove so good and got us here safe and sound. I don't think a crash would have been very nice."

We got checked into two nice rooms, same floor, and Susan agreed that was by far the most elegant hotel she had ever seen. We strolled around the grounds for an hour or two and then to our rooms. I luxuriated in the tub, since I have only a shower at home. We met for dinner about eight o'clock and enjoyed a delicious meal. She settled for a small tenderloin steak, and I chose veal cutlets. The appearance of an elderly white man and a beautiful young black girl caused no raised eyebrows. In the room, a phone message said the audition would be at the nearby Gaslight Theater at ten the next morning. That is where Music City Tonight comes on five nights a week. I told Susan I would breakfast early, and call her at eight, to give her two hours to get a bit to eat and get ready. She smiled sort of thinly and said okay.

Up at six, and another moment of pure joy soaking in the tub. This was late January, and Nashville has been known to have some hellish winter weather this time of year. Since I didn't have to audition, I pigged out again on ham and eggs, red eye gravy, hot biscuits, and honey. I called Susan at eight, told her of the tasty breakfast and she could have the same if she hurried, but she said a couple of pieces of whole wheat toast and a big glass of milk would be all she could handle.

A little before ten, we walked into the Gaslight Theater by the back door, just as Lorianne and Charlie were arriving. Jim Owens was already present.

I said rather proudly, "Folks, meet Miss Susan Sanders of Boise, Idaho. Susan, this is Mr. Owens and Lorianne and Charlie."

Susan beamed and shook hands with each.

She was calm and collected and confident, and exclaimed at once. "Let's get started. I've got a pretty new Tennessee song to sing."

She settled herself at the piano bench, and that magical voice filled the 600-seat auditorium, now totally empty. She grinned at the finish, and turned around to see Jim Owens and Charlie and Lorianne with ear-to-ear smiles and nearly speechless.

Lorianne recovered to say, "Susan, that was as beautiful a song that you sang as I've ever heard, and your voice made it so special. We heard your tape, and you are even better in person."

Charlie seemed stunned, but gave the two thumbs up sign. Jim Owens was open-mouthed, his face alive with admiration and appreciation.

"Miss Sanders, would you like to be on Music City Tonight in about a month?" Susan was almost crying, but almost shouted YES!

Then Susan looked at me, and I wasted no time. She got that bear hug I had either threatened or promised, and I do believe I felt a slight hug in return. At that blissful moment, I knew Susan and I would become lifelong friends, with complete trust in each other.

That was a rare moment and day of total happiness, and I believe Susan felt the same way. I found myself choking down a big lump in my throat. Lorianne gave Susan a big hug; Charlie put an arm around her in congratulations, and Mr. Owens shook her hands vigorously.

Susan was on her way.

I brought everybody down to earth by asking Mr. Owens how many songs Susan would sing on her opening night.

Owens: "Two would be perfect for her first appearance. What will be your second song, Susan?"

Susan looked at me, and we both nodded our heads. She turned around and made the piano come to life again. She belted out "Sunny Side Up," which also said, hide the side that gets blue, and finished with a pulsating flourish.

Again, Lorianne was wide-eyed, and asked if I had written that song, too.

I told her no, that it was from an early-day talking movie, either in the late 20s or early 30s. I thought, but was not sure, that Janet Gaynor had sung the song, and I thought, but again was not sure, that the name of the movie was "Street Angels."

They all looked at me as if I were an old historic relic for remembering that far back, and they were right.

Then I asked Mr. Owens what Susan would be paid, and he thought for a moment and offered, "She will get $1,500 which is above scale, but Susan is so talented she will get a little bonus. I merely said I thought $2,000 would be nicer and reminded Mr. Owens that he had agreed to pay the travel expenses for Susan and me if she were accepted for Music City Tonight. He nodded and said sure and added that our expenses also would be paid every time Susan was on the show.

MUSIC CITY TONIGHT IS NEXT

A date was set for a Monday night, a month off. Then we told all of them we had to get to a phone and call Susan's folks with the good news.

Mr. Owens looked at his watch, which said eleven, and said it was a very special occasion, and we should have lunch at noon in the hotel dining room.

We tore back to the hotel, took the elevator to the fifth floor, and Susan started fumbling with the phone in my room. She was so nervous she handed me the phone and I punched out the 208/376 and the last four numbers. I handed the phone back to Susan, who cried out, "Oh, Mamma, I made it, and I'm going to be on Music City Tonight." Then she started bawling, and gave the phone back to me, but mumbled, "Dougie, give me your handkerchief." That was the first of several hankies that I lost, never to be seen again. But they went to a wonderful cause.

I told Gloria how well she had done, that we would be home late the next afternoon, and to see if she could persuade Eric to have a bottle of Heineken's cold when we got there. Gloria laughed and said she was sure Eric would have a bottle of my favorite beer.

We met Jim, Lorianne, and Charlie in the dining room and Elaine, the secretary, came along. Lorianne and Elaine ordered, and Jim asked Susan what she would like. "Well, if it's not too late, I'll have ham and eggs and red eye gravy and hot biscuits and honey." I grinned, and Jim said that sounded great, he'd have the same thing. I settled for a ham sandwich.

Jim asked Susan if she liked the kind of food she had ordered, and Susan answered demurely, "First time I've ever tried it, but Doug had it for breakfast and said it was the best meal ever. I was too nervous to eat anything, but now I'm hungry." Susan ate with gusto, smacked her lips and said she would have it every time she came to Nashville.

We drifted back to our rooms, and as we were getting off the elevator, Susan stopped abruptly, turned to me and said in a dismayed voice, "Did you realize I went right into your room before lunch and we were there all by ourselves? I can't figure what's coming over me."

I replied as soothingly as I could, "No big deal. We were just acing natural, and I imagine we will be in the same room together a lot of times. Now, I'm going to get my thirty minutes of beauty sleep, and I think a nap would refresh you, too. Why don't I call you in a hour, and we'll see some of Nashville."

Susan said okay, and that is what happened. A cab took us on a fairly brief tour. We saw where the Grand Old Opry was held, and we learned this was the 70th anniversary of that widely-loved event. We also saw the state capitol and downtown areas. Nashville was a bustling city, but there was a smog problem.

Later in the afternoon, we continued our inspection of Opryland Hotel, and all its features and attractions impressed both of us deeply.

A delicious dinner, up the next morning for the return flight home, and we upgraded to first class since Music City Tonight was paying the tab. Susan took an hour nap between Chicago and Boise, and when we landed, Susan took a big breath and just said she was thankful we hadn't crashed.

I asked her in all seriousness not to call me Dougie in public, but that it was all right in private, and that my mother was the only other person who had ever called me that. Susan smiled tenderly, and said of course.

We got to Susan's house about five-thirty, and Eric is a dang good man, as witness the fact that he had a twelve pack of Heineken's.

After hugs and kisses for Susan, and a pretty good squeeze for me from Gloria and Sally and a firm handshake from Eric, we opened a bottle of beer.

When we were all seated, Susan got up, looked loftily around the room, and pronounced dramatically, "My deah people, ahrn't you all glad and proud to have such a famous star as little ol' me in your family. Aftuh all, I will bring fame and fortune to the Sanders family." She kept going in an outrageous "Bahston" accent until Sally snorted and told Susan to quit being such a ham.

Susan laughed merrily and nearly sat in my lap, then

moved to one side but kept hooking her arm through mine. Eric and Gloria smiled in approval.

Eric asked Sally and Susan if they wanted a taste of his beer, and they both sniffed disdainfully and said no, they did not drink that hog slop. Eric and I looked at each other, both thinking the same thing—the younger generation simply does not appreciate the finer things in life.

I made the motion that we go out to dinner to celebrate, drink, and be merry. I asked Eric if he was able to drive after two beers. He just retorted, "Get in, I can handle this here critter." It was a Jeep Cherokee and indeed handled us all very well.

There is a rather elegant dining room at the Red Lion Riverside, and that is where he headed. Another bottle of Heineken's made Eric and me feel much better. Gloria had a glass of wine, Sally a Diet Coke, and Susan said she would have a straight shot—then grinned and said 7-UP. We all ate heartily.

The Jeep with Eric as pilot got us home safe and sound, and I walked to the door with them. Suddenly, Susan grabbed my arm and almost wailed, "I'm scared to death," obviously thinking ahead three weeks when she would make her debut on Music City Tonight.

I merely said, "I'm scared, too. Let's go in for a minute and I'll tell you why." We sat down in the living room and I commenced to Susan, "I bet you a thousand to one those people would like your tape. I bet you ten thousand to one they would like your audition. Now I'll bet you a hundred thousand to one that you will be one of the greatest newcomers ever to go to Nashville.

"What I'm scared about is that I didn't inspect the ceiling in the theater. The people are going to be clapping their hands so loud, that ceiling will probably go up three or four feet, and I don't want it falling down on the audience.

"Susan, I can tell you this, you are going to be a big star, and in three weeks it will just be the start. You just believe that, and it will come true. Okay?" Susan almost cried, but gave me a big hug, while Eric, Gloria, and Sally smiled happily.

THE ICEBERG STARTS TO MELT

After I left, Susan sat with her parents and asked almost in wonder, "Mamma, how come I think so much of a white man? He's the first one who has never hassled me; he's kind and gentle and treats me like a lady all the time. He didn't try to get fresh when we went to Nashville, and pretty soon I knew he was not going to make a play for me."

Sally interrupted and asked saucily, "You falling in love with him?"

Susan answered slowly and thoughtfully. "No, but I'm sure starting to think the world of him. You noticed how he told me there was no reason to be scared about going back to Nashville? He's always taking care of me and that is why I truly like him. Maybe I'm starting to love him, but not to be IN love with him.

"He hints sometimes that he is four times as old as me, and I wonder how he can have such a youngish look if he is that old. He told me about a book by Art Linkletter called *Old Age Ain't for Sissies* and he said he would never be a sissy, and I believe him. He told me he had five granddaughters, a grandson, and a great grandson, and just thinking about them and being with them kept him thinking young."

Eric, Gloria, and Sally all gave Susan a big hug. They had listened with respect, and said they all like Doug, too, implying that Susan's regards for me was surely okay with them.

The next morning, my phone rang and it was Gloria, Susan's mother, and she sounded serious from the start. She asked if she could come by for a few minutes, and of course I said sure. A few minutes later, she arrived, came in, and sat on the couch.

"I have to talk to you, because I believe Susan is commencing to believe in you as a friend and you must never do anything to hurt her."

My response: "Mrs. Sanders, Susan already has a very warm spot in my heart, and I want only the best for her. I would never hurt her in any way."

SUSAN'S MISFORTUNES

Mrs. Sanders hesitated a moment, then said, "You are entitled to know why Susan treated you so badly. Let me tell you why. Susan was hit by polio when she was just seven years old. We lived in San Antonio where Eric was stationed at the Air Force base. We moved to Spokane and then Mountain Home Air Force Base soon after that, and Susan started going to a physical therapist twice a week. One day she came home crying and when I asked her why, she said the young therapist, not a member of the Air Force, had pulled up her dress. She said, "He tried to stick his finger in my wee-wee hole, and I fell off the table. He got scared and told me not to tell anybody about this.'

"That night," Mrs. Sanders continued, "I told Eric. There are times in dealing with Air Force brats that he can get sort of mad. This time, his face turned cold and he said he would take care of the matter in the morning. I know he was fuming on the inside. Eric had been in the Air Force for twenty years, and he was respected by officers and enlisted men and women alike. He was top sergeant when he retired four years ago.

"The next morning, Eric was in a cold rage. He told the base commanding officer what had happened, and what he intended to do, which was to beat the hell out of that young therapist. I'm sure he used stronger words than that. His CO told Eric he had his approval to take proper action.

"Eric found the young man in his office, lifted him up by his shirt front, and then told him he had thirty minutes to disappear, that the next time Eric saw him, he would take the young man apart piece by piece, slow and hurtful. The CO was standing at the door, and warned the young man to get going and not come back. The young therapist was terrified, and was gone when Eric came back.

"I thought grimly that if this young punk ever showed up again, Eric would put a real hurt on him."

Mrs. Sanders continued her account of Susan's life, including a dramatic confrontation with the polio doctor who told Susan, with regret in his voice, that Susan would not be able to walk again on account of the polio.

Gloria said Susan narrowed her eyes, practically growled at the doctor, and told him to his face he didn't know what he was talking about, and that she would walk again, even if it took years and years of rehabilitation. Susan looked mad enough to spit in the doctor's eye, Gloria recounted. Susan spent two years in a wheelchair, two years on a walker, two years on crutches, and two years with a cane, which she threw away angrily one day. Eric found an old-fashioned therapist in Mountain Home, and he told Susan if she did hundreds of certain exercises a day, those atrophied muscles in her left leg might regain some strength. Susan's complete dedication and motivation had gotten her to the point where the limp was scarcely noticeable, but she continued her exercises.

Another unhappy event took place when Susan was

16; again it involved a civilian therapist at the base. She saw him occasionally, but one time the civilian tried to run his hand up Susan's dress. She bit his hand hard, backhanded him, and limped out on her cane. Eric heard the story that night, called on the young man the next morning, grabbed him by the shirt and slapped him a few times. "You have thirty minutes to get off the base. If you're still here when I come back, you're likely not to live very long."

Again this second young man vanished for good.

Gloria summed up, "Those two unhappy bits in Susan's life left her hating all white men, although she knew the whities couldn't all be bad. But that is why Susan was so cold to you. Now, though, she is happier than she has ever been, and I know it is because she has come to trust you. She said last night after you left that she felt close to you, so please don't ever let her down."

"Mrs. Sanders," I said slowly, "somehow Susan has become real precious to me. I wouldn't do anything to hurt your daughter. She has a great future and I think she and I make a real good team."

Mrs. Sanders just smiled and responded, "I am glad Susan met you and know you will take good care of her."

WONDERFUL MIRACLE

An elderly white man and a beautiful young black girl, that's what had developed in just a few weeks. I pondered that situation a lot these days, knowing it was a rare happening, but having a gut feeling that Susan and I had become firm friends and that friendship would continue to grow.

Several days passed, and one morning the phone sounded, and it was Susan's by now familiar voice.

She started off, "Mr. B, I'm worried about that ceiling at the Gaslight Theater. Would you please tell me some more about it?"

"If tomorrow is your afternoon off, would you do me the honor of having lunch?" I responded.

Susan came back with, "I'll clear my social calendar and be in front of the Performing Arts Building at high noon. That okay?"

It was, so at noon, Susan was right on time. I opened the car door for her without a protest, and we lunched at Peg Leg Annie's, named for a legendary pioneer woman who suffered amputation of both legs after struggling through a long march in a blizzard. Peg Leg also was remembered as being the madame of one of the first cat houses in the area. The place is very friendly, the food and service excellent, and there are several hundred thousands of dollars' worth of antiques on every wall. Susan hadn't seen the memorabilia, so we drifted from room to room examining the displays, then back to the annex where smoking is permitted and where the bar is located.

Susan wanted to know what was good, so I told her one of my favorites was the halibut fish and chips, and we both ordered that tasty dish.

We lingered over coffee, and I realized I knew nothing of Susan's early life.

"Didn't I tell you I was born in San Antonio? she asked. "Daddy had finished high school and enlisted in the Air Force when he was 18, because he didn't have any money to go to college. He met Mama at some meeting on the air base near San Antone, they fell in love and got married on his Air Force pay, which wasn't very much. I was born in 1974 after they'd been married about three years, and then we moved to the air base near Spokane. When I was six, he was transferred to Mountain Home. Mama finished her college work at Gonzaga in Spokane, getting a BA in English and history. When we moved to Boise, Daddy took mail courses from Boise State, but it took him six years to get a degree in economics.

"Daddy had been promoted on a regular basis, and turned down a chance to go to officer's training school. He was top sergeant, and everybody liked him and respected him. He retired four years ago, and gets a decent pension. And he has a fine job at Hewlett-Packard here in Boise, and Mama is in demand as a substitute teacher, so we can pay the mortgage every month. We moved to Boise four years ago, and I sure like living here. I don't make many friends, but there are a few of the gals I like to hang out with.

"Goshamighty," she exclaimed, "I've yakked too much, but I feel like we are becoming good friends, and I like that, and appreciate it."

We left about one-thirty and went to her home, and she said I had to come in for awhile to think of new ways to calm her nerves.

"Madam," I opened, "when those big doors open, you'll be standing by the piano ready to sit down and sing. Just try to take a look at that ceiling, because about five minutes later it will start to rise a little bit from all the applause you are going to get. You are normal and human like everybody else, you'll be a bit nervous to start; but sweetie, you have a thrilling voice, you are very pretty and I'll bet you a million to one everybody will love you."

She smiled as if she were glad that I had all that confidence in her, murmured thanks, said she felt better and was anxious to get to Nashville and sing that pretty Tennessee song.

Time Drags On

The last week before Susan's big night dragged by agonizingly slow, but if Susan was worried, it didn't show. We had lunch twice, once at Marie Callender's and once at the Red Robin, and there was nothing the matter with her appetite. She had a continual slight smile on her face, and was polite enough to giggle if I tried to pop a corny. She knew I was trying to cheer her up, but her confident look make it clear that any phony attempt on my part was not needed.

She bought a couple of elegant slacks outfits, and I even splurged myself with a new suit, the first one in a long time and probably the last I would ever buy. We were going to be a well-dressed couple.

I even went downtown to the Idaho Potato Commission offices and got a sackful of the little Idaho potato pins, which are free for the first 100. The lady in charge reckoned that at least five million of the little brown souvenirs had been given away in the last twenty or twenty-five years.

So Sunday morning finally came. I picked Susan up at six forty-five and we headed for the airport with the echoes of well wishes and hugs and kisses for Susan and hearty handshakes for me. It was late February, 1994.

We settled into first class seats and let the friendly skies take us to Chicago and then on to Nashville by late afternoon. Susan had practically ordered me to tell the pilot to drive carefully. She grinned, "I may not let my full weight down until we land." She was totally in command of herself.

The Opryland bus got us to the hotel about five. Susan's orders were a medium size walk, inside and out, although the weatherman was blundering and the thunder was rumbling. At seven thirty it was Heineken time, then a delicious dinner of prime ribs, another walk to settle our meal, and to bed by ten thirty.

I called Susan at eight the next morning, and she said to wait on her for breakfast. Her healthy appetite was not going to be ignored, and she ordered—you guessed it—ham and eggs and red eye gravy and hot biscuits and honey. She patted her stomach delicately, and made a mocking scowl, and spoke vigorously, "Lemme at 'em, I'm ready to go." I grinned a wide grin.

Rehearsal was at ten-thirty and Susan sang her songs like a champion. Jim Owens and Lorianne and Charlie gave her big thumbs ups. I made a special call on Wanda, whom I think is the best fiddler in the country, to pay special attention to the parts of the song where harmony adds greatly to the singing. Wanda was perfect. I wondered to myself if Wanda had ever heard of Uncle Jimmy Johnson, an early-day Grand Ol' Opry pioneer who made a fiddle sit up and talk. Uncle Jimmy said he always trained hard to play his fiddle, with a supply of white lightning moonshine to grease his arms.

Susan declined lunch, with only a glass of milk and a green salad, and I settled for a tuna fish sandwich.

Then the long wait, until taping of tonight's show at five o'clock.

I called for Susan at four. She opened the door, and she started strutting around the room, spinning and showing off in her new outfit.

I couldn't help it. I clapped my hands and told her, "My God, lady, you are dazzling and beautiful and besides that, you are pretty, too."

Susan beamed, and we headed for the dressing rooms where the final touches would be applied for Susan. They figured I was too unimportant and impossible to beautify and doll-up, so I snuck a cigarette in a prohibited area, said a little prayer for Susan's success, and then just waited.

I strolled outside, and the February sun, although not warm, was cool and refreshing. I reflected what a lucky old buzzard I was. An aging white man being associated with a beautiful young black girl was hard to analyze. Susan was a slender five-foot-three with the curves in the right places, rather wiry in spite of her weak left leg, but she had steel in her spine. I thanked my lucky stars at my good fortune, and went back inside.

If it were possible, Susan looked even lovelier and more attractive. There were still fifteen minutes before she went on, and she suddenly grabbed my arm and blurted out, "Dougie, I'm scared!"

I heaved a sigh of relief which she heard and saw, and I just said to her "Thank goodness. I'd have worried if you hadn't been scared. Now you know you are human and worrying is just being natural. Now I KNOW you will be sensational. All you have to do is let your voice take over and then start wondering how far the ceiling will rise. Sweetie, you're going to be great."

She giggled, took a deep breath and I could see some fire starting to glint in her eyes, so I knew she would be wonderful. She gave some stern orders.

Her directive: "When I finish that song, you be close by. You'll probably have to hold me up."

"My little sugar plum, I will be there," I told her.

Time for Susan to walk out behind those massive doors, which swung open as Doc Damon presented Susan with enthusiasm. "Now, ladies and gentlemen, please welcome Miss Susan Sanders of Boise, Idaho."

Susan was standing by the piano, gazing out at a full house of 600 in the audience, unable to see them because of the bright spotlight on her.

SUSAN TRIUMPHS

She sat down, nodded to Buddy Skipper, and the strains of that Tennessee song started to unfold. Then Susan just let her voice take command. Those pure, piercing notes came from her throat like the voice of an angel, and she immediately continued with full confidence. The song poured forth, and the harmony with Wanda blended perfectly with the words "purple hills when day is done." As the last words of the song trailed off, there was almost a reverent silence. Then the crowd erupted with thunderous applause, lots of approving whistles, and hands clapping as they had never clapped before. Susan stood up as if mesmerized, then gave a sweeping bow and blew a kiss to the people. She seemed to sway just slightly, and then I slipped to her side, whispering "Sweetie, you were perfect." She took my arm and I told her softly to blow more kisses, and soon we were across the stage where Lorianne and Charlie were waiting, and they were both applauding. When the applause finally died down, Susan and I took our seats on the couch, and I spoke into my chest mike, "Lorianne and Charlie and folks, I think you will agree a star is born."

The 600 agreed and continued to clap vigorously.

Lorianne and Charlie were almost speechless, but they both said almost with reverence, "Susan, you were sensational." Charlie added, "We have had hundreds of stars on this show, but none of them got the applause you have received. And you deserved it, too, because I have never heard a more beautiful voice. It is an honor for Music City Tonight to introduce you to the rest of the country."

Susan sat there, shaking her head in wonder at the acclamation, and whispered, "Doug, give me your handkerchief," and she wept silently.

"Those are tears of happiness, folks," Lorianne declared.

And they were. Susan regained control and spoke firmly into her mike, "Folks, I thank all of you from the bottom of my heart." She kept the hanky and used it again.

Lorianne couldn't wait to start asking questions.

"I've got to know how you two became acquainted. You seem to be a wonderful team. What happened?"

Susan took over and started laughing.

"Lorianne, I don't like to use this word, but I've just got to tell you that I knocked Doug on his ass the first time we met." Lorrianne's hand went to her mouth as if she couldn't believe what she just heard. Charlie reared back, mystified, too.

Susan continued, "At Boise State, our professor, Dr. Schroeder, had four girls in to sing that new Tennessee song that Doug wrote. I was late getting there, but heard one of the girls sing it, and I knew I wanted to try it, too. Doug was standing by the piano, so I told him to play it, and he did and hit a lot of sour notes. I thought to myself this guy needs piano lessons. Then I told him to let me try it, and I sat down on the piano bench, and told him to scoot over. I scooted him too hard, and he slipped off the bench and landed on his rear end. He sat there laughing, and the girls helped him up and asked him if he was hurt. He patted himself on his backside and said no, he had landed on his brains. Then he pointed at me, and said, 'Young lady, you are the first girl in fifty years to knock me on my ass.'"

The crowd howled, and Lorianne and Charlie both winced, but joined in the laughter.

After the taping was finished, everybody on the show told Susan how great she was and what a pleasure it was to work with her.

Jim Owens asked to speak to Susan and me in a

corner, and said straight out, "Susan, we'd like you to come back in May, September, and December. Can you do it?"

Susan burst out with "I sure can."

I asked Jim what Susan's fee would be, and he said $2,500 and then $3,500. I suggested that $3,000 and $5,000 sounded better. He hesitated, so I interjected "If you can borrow or buy the tape from Susan's song today, and let her use it for a single video, she can accept a lower fee."

Jim immediately said "Fine. I can get the tape at a reasonable cost, and probably find you a producer to make the video, and probably make you a lot of money."

Jim was as good as his word. His clout with TNN got a very good, not too expensive deal, and he found a new production company, Smoky Mountain Productions, to make the video. The bosses at Smoky Mountain had heard Susan sing, and they agreed to do the video with no money down. We agreed on a certain number of videos to be sold before the company got its investment back, and after that we would all share in the profit, if indeed there were any profits to be had.

The long running miracle extended itself. Susan's video took off sky high, and quickly sold 300,000 copies the first ninety days. The producer said he was confident it would hit gold in another sixty days, which is 500,000 copies sold.

So, Susan and I each earned a good chunk of dough, in keeping with our agreement made in front of her folks earlier, that we would split fifty-fifty on songs that I wrote and songs that she sung.

On Top of Cloud Nine

Needless to say, we were on Cloud Nine. Susan, being a normal woman, went on a shopping spree, buying fine gifts for her parents and sister. I was grateful that at long last I could set up college trust funds for four grandkids and a great grandson.

A couple of weeks after our return from Susan's triumphant debut on Music City Tonight, she asked casually what songs I would recommend for her second time around.

I told her I'd like for her to hear an old time favorite titled "I Want To Be a Cowboy's Sweetheart," and that I had it on a cassette at home. There we went after lunch and Susan showed great excitement at the song. She called a couple of days later and gave me orders again.

"You send word to Jim Owens that I want a complete cowgirl's outfit when I sing that cute song. I want shirt, Levis, vest, chaps, a lasso rope, two holsters, and two six guns in 'em. This is going to be a dang blasted good stunt."

Then she asked about her second song, and I said one of my favorite hymns was "Just a Closer Walk With Thee," and would that suit her? She said "Oh Yes, it is one of my favorites, too. We have it in a hymnal here at the house and I will love to do it."

Well, mere words cannot describe Susan's second starry time in Nashville.

She warbled "Cowboy Sweetheart," and yodeled like a top Swiss pro. Buddy Skipper had a cute arrangement of the song, and Susan hit the jackpot.

She had a medley of cowboy songs, and included "Ragtime Cowboy Joe," and "Empty Saddles." When she finished, the crowd roared with pleasure. Then Susan called out, "Cowboy, throw me my rope." She caught it easily and she put on a dazzling display of roping tricks, twirling it behind her, above her, up and down and sideways, and when through, casually tossed the rope a few feet and caught it as it settled on her arm. The crowd again almost went wild. They all loved this little gal from Boise.

Susan stepped back to the mike, and uttered these words, "If it wasn't for this dang-blasted leg, I'd be hoppin' and skippin' and jumpin', and I'll betcha I'll be able to do those things in a year." She made a wide, sweeping bow to the audience.

Then she hooked her thumbs in her Levis, swaggered over toward the couch. Before she sat down, she had the crowd cheering louder and louder.

She said this, in the most outrageous Southern drawl ever invented, "Ah'm tellin' you all, that from now on Ah'm gonna be a good ol' Southern gal. I ain't never gonna be a gorgeous Southern Belle like Lorianne, but Ah'm a aimin' to try to be a sweet little ol' gal from south of the Mason Dixon. You all bettah remembah that." With that, she strutted to her seat and plopped down, blowing on her fingers and rubbing them across her chest like comic braggarts do. The crowd ate it all up, and the hand clapping echoed for several minutes.

Lorianne and Charlie had been watching in amazement and admiration at all the talent Susan was displaying and they were standing and applauding.

As she sat down, Susan leaned over and asked me, "How'd I do, Podnah?"

I whispered back, "You are a bigger ham than Bob Hope." She seemed pleased to be in such distinguished company.

The crowd demanded an encore. Susan got up, swaggering again, and then said, "You all bettah remember Ah'm an ol' cowhand from the Rio Grande. From now on Ah's carryin' my two guns, and I ain't gonna take any back talk from anybody. Ah'm full of spit and vinegar, Ah'm ruff and tuff and hard to bluff, and I can whup a passle of wildcats and coyotes."

Charlie and Lorianne were doubled over with laughter at Susan's encore. She got a couple of drum rolls and the crash of a cymbal from the band. Susan had gained a permanent spot in the hearts of all those who were there and tuned into TNN. This gal with such amazing versatility could croon, warble, do the blues, yodel, do a mean honky tonk and that unforgettable voice placed her at new levels of entertainment. Indeed, she was one in a million.

Later for her second number, she was dressed in a white robe and gown. She announced quietly that her song was to be one of her favorite hymns. She sang "Just a Closer Walk With Thee" like an angel. The audience was almost worshipful, and gave tremendous, though somewhat restrained, applause.

There was no doubt in anyone's mind that Susan was on her way to becoming a major star.

She still had her feet on the ground. That night, over dinner, she suddenly said, "Yum, yum. I can hardly wait for my favorite breakfast." And the next morning, she devoured a huge meal of ham and eggs and red eye gravy, several hot biscuits and honey, and even a small portion of grits.

She grinned as she swallowed the last bite. "Ah reckon Ah'm gettin' to be a regular old Southern gal, ain't I?"

BACK TO BOISE

On the trip to Chicago, I told her next time I'd like to get us two rooms with a connecting door. She could keep her side locked and I'd do the same. Then if we needed each other, all it would take would be a knock on the door. It beat going out into the hall and walking to each other's room. She said that would be a lot more convenient, then added, quite gravely, "I made up my mind weeks ago that you were not ever going to hurt me or insult me. You see, I trust you completely now."

That statement consolidated us as a first-class team, with trust in each other.

After a pretty good airline lunch out of Chicago, Susan dozed off. I was sort of dozing, too, when my thoughts started straying to some of the events in my life, concentrating on the good thoughts and letting the not-so-good remain in the not-to-be-remembered category.

In the mid-thirties, I was assistant sports editor of the old *Knoxville Journal,* now long deceased. I was assigned to cover the Tennessee-Long Island basketball game in the old Madison Square Garden, and the next morning hitched a ride to Pompton Lakes, New Jersey, where Joe Louis was training for a fight, I believe against Bob Pastor. I watched Joe shooting pool at one of the tables, when this likeable world heavyweight boxing champ looked up and said with a friendly smile, "Grab a stick and I'll whup you good." I went for half a game with the champ before he was called away to do some more training.

Later, as sports editor of the *Press-Chronicle* in Johnson City, Tennessee, I played a game of gin rummy with Jack Dempsey, the former champ, who was travelling with a circus. In that high-pitched voice after the first game, he advised me that I owed him a dime, which I paid in cash.

After living in Pocatello in 1942 and working as the general manager of the Pocatello Cardinals, a farm club of the St. Louis Cards in the then Class C Pioneer League, I was grabbed by the Navy in the summer of 1943, and sent to the west and southwest Pacific six months later. For a few months I was a bootlegger on a little island called Emirau. The then Major Joe Foss, who was to become the Marine's first ace by shooting down five Japanese planes, was commander of a Marine Air Wing on Emirau. A nearby Seabee construction battalion had numerous craftsmen, who made ash trays, belt buckles, and other clever items from the metal of a Japanese plane which had been shot down. We paid six dollars to the Seabee men, then swapped the souvenirs to the Joe Foss pilots for bottles of rum and whiskey, which we then sold for about seventy-five dollars. That profitable operation lasted only a few months, but I did accumulate a few bucks to send home to my wife, who had given birth to our first son.

Joe Foss himself was a much decorated war hero, who later became governor of South Dakota, then was president of the old American Football League.

The Emirau story had more to go. Charles Lindbergh, who for a few years was a peace-nik and severely criticized for his appeasement of Hitler and the Germans, visited on Emirau while we were there, and I have two valuable, prized possessions from Lindbergh's visit. I have a short snorter dollar bill autographed by Lindbergh and Foss. I took a splendid picture of them striding in camp. The picture and autographed bill are in a safe place and if anyone is interested in buying them, the bidding starts at $25,000.

Lindbergh was reliably reported to have flown combat missions with the Marines, and I know he took a PT scouting trip down towards New Guinea because I made the trip on the same PT boat the next night, and the crew told of how friendly Lindbergh was.

After the war, we moved to Twin Falls and I worked for the Idaho American Legion for a couple of years. One mission was to Sun Valley where President Harry Truman and staff and cabinet officers were having a conference. I got there in time to watch a softball game among cabinet members and the press. The President was also a spectator, and the then Secretary of State General George Marshall was umpire. A photographer was kind enough to take a picture of me shaking hands with President Truman, and that photo now hangs proud on a wall at home.

Still dozing and letting my thoughts stray back a good number of years, I grinned inwardly at two happenings, one favorable and the other rather unfavorable.

In the late 1930s, as I have said earlier, as sports editor of the *Press-Chronicle* at John City, I covered football, basketball, and other sports at what was then East Tennessee State Teachers College. Having written about football, I decided to go out for football to get a first-hand taste of the game, which was rather brutal even in the long ago.

I became the 33rd man on a 33-man football squad. I wrote a sports column that the last man on the squad was important because he had to work harder and learn a lot more about the game. I joked that my place on the squad gave me the name of Judge Bradford, because I spent so much time on the bench. Somehow, the president of the college, whose name has faded from memory, and who taught a Sunday morning class at church, saw something inspiring in the column and used it as the text of his next meeting, that even the last man in line works hard to keep the men ahead of him bearing down to do their best. I was very, very flattered.

Years later, in 1948 and living in Twin Falls, I was hired by the incumbent mayor and city councilmen who were up for reelection, to write press articles and speeches for them. Twin Falls had approved slot machines a couple of years earlier. Even though it was widely believed that the slot operators were connected with the mobs and their gangsters, the city had received hundreds of thousands of dollars from the machines, and used the revenue to build a new city swimming pool, install street lights, new baseball park, and other benefits.

Reelection of the mayor and councilmen seemed a cinch—but a few weeks before election, the publisher of the daily *Times News* and prominent business leaders got together and decided that the slots had to go.

Pastors preached against the evils of gambling and slot machines, and the minister of my own Methodist church named me and the mayor and councilmen as corrupters of the public morals, and we lost the election.

I opened my eyes slowly, and the flight attendant came by with a big smile that was genuine. "We'll be landing in fifteen minutes, and you may want to wake Miss Sanders up," she said.

"Thank you ma'am, I'll do just that." I returned and Shook Susan gently and whispered, "Wake up, little angel, we're going to be back on earth pretty soon." Susan's big brown eyes opened, and she was lovely.

"Scuse me, Podnah, I gotta go to the john." She came back, fresh looking, and we sat together waiting for the plane to land, which it did safely.

Later, as we rode to her house, I thought ruefully to myself that I had done too much thinking and reminiscing about myself. Susan was the story and the glory of my life.

I added one thought to my inner rumblings. I had lost the Twin Falls city election, but in 1950 I was redeemed, helping to elect a U.S. senator, a governor, and two congressmen, all Republicans. So I evened my won/lost record to .500.

VIDEO SALES ZOOM

After Susan's second appearance in Nashville, sales of her video jumped strongly, going over 500,000, and she and I enjoyed another healthy check.

One night when I called for Susan to take to dinner, she was a couple of minutes late, and came down the stairs when ready. I couldn't help from exclaiming, "My gosh, you are gorgeous." She gave me a big hug, and without thinking I asked her this, "Susan, would you do me the honor of being my honorary granddaughter?"

Her eyes lit up like moonbeams and she cried, "Oh, yes!" Then she started bawling and said plaintively, "Dougie, give me your handkerchief." So there went another handkerchief, but she was radiantly happy, managing to get the words out "now we really belong to each other."

That was a rare moment of happiness for me.

Then to get her to stop crying, I told her semi-sternly that now that she was my granddaughter, she would have to mind me and obey all orders.

Her tears stopped and with a little glint in her eyes, she advised me thusly, "Podnah, I'll obey anything that only I like, and I will not be at your wish and command." Then I was rewarded with another huge hug.

We had an unusually pleasant time at dinner that night.

On the way home, she said she just happened to be wondering what songs she would sing for her September date in Nashville. I told her I had a couple of sweet songs for her to hear, and if she came by in the morning, I would entertain her on my Yamaha organ keyboard.

She showed up at ten and went directly to the keyboard, which was on my kitchen table covered by a towel.

She was in an ordering mood, so she commanded, "Let's hear the songs."

I had been practicing regularly, so I played them. One was what I thought was a pretty love song that went like this.

> Sunset and evening star above,
> Bring mem'ries of the one I love;
> I swear to you I will always be
> Faithful and true thru eternity;
> We'll build our mem'ries as years go by,
> Wonderful dreams come true,
> Together we'll share perfect happiness,
> I give my love to you.

Again, just reading the words makes hearing the tune impossible, but Susan was excited and said she loved the song and wanted to sing it in Nashville. Then she asked about my second number, and it was a lullaby.

> Time to close your eyes and sleep,
> Little sleepyhead;
> Angels wait to guard and keep,
> Little sleepyhead;
> Sandman's waiting now for you,
> So dream of playmates all night thru;
> Now I lay you down to sleep,
> Little sleepyhead.

Susan looked at me and said some real nice words, "Podnah, you sure do write pretty songs, and I want to do both of them." Later, we would figure out a more peppy number for her third song, and I gave her Xerox copies of "I Give My Love to You" and "Little Sleepyhead" which names I had given to my two outputs.

I lit a cigarette, and Susan fussed and fumed,

41

charging that I smoked too much. Then we got up and went into the living room, and for the first time noticed my mantle pictures and also the elegant pieces of driftwood. "You have a handsome family and I want to meet all of them," she said firmly. I agreed, and we talked of a trip to Gooding, Idaho, just one hundred miles down the pike where my son Dave and wife and three kids live. Dave is pastor of the Gooding Methodist Church and the members love him. Doug and Steve live in California, and we put that on a future schedule. Greg and family live in Minneapolis, and maybe we could stop there for a day or two on the way back from Nashville.

Susan's eyes lit up. "By gosh," she opined, "that's where the world's largest shopping mall is located, and I see no reason why we couldn't stay a couple of weeks while I check that place out."

She kept on inspecting the house, with three small bedrooms, bath and a half, small kitchen, and a tiny breakfast nook. She asked if she could open the refrigerator, and I told her to go ahead. Inside was a large bottle of 7-UP, and she practically glowed as she lifted it out.

Then she added, "Nope, it's too early in the day for me to drink, but I'm sure glad to know that bottle is there." She didn't mention the bottles of Heineken's.

She asked no questions about my driftwood display, for I was prepared to brag that I used to be the No. 1 driftwood hunter in Idaho. Maybe I'll tell her later, and do a little boasting about the choice pieces that I have found.

Before she left, she suddenly said she would like to do "Stand By Your Man" as her third song in September. I agreed happily, for Tammy Wynette was absolutely unforgettable when she introduced it quite a few years back.

To Nashville Again

We were practically old-timers heading for Nashville in mid-September. Susan had registered for her senior year at Boise State, and was a cinch to graduate with honors. She even let her full weight down during the flight.

As usual, Susan continued to get roaring approval for her three songs, and bless her heart, she told the folks I had written two of them. When she sang "Stand By Your Man" with a thrilling performance, she paid generous tribute to Tammy, and I hope Tammy was listening.

Jim Owens, Lorianne, and Charlie got us to one side after the show, and asked Susan if December 18 would suit her to be a part of an all-star Christmas version of Music City Tonight. "Oh, sure," Susan replied merrily. "That's during the holidays and it will be a great break for us with no school to worry about."

Lorianne said she would like Susan to sing "Silent Night" and Susan was thrilled to sing her favorite Christmas carol. Lorianne said Reba, Vince, Tammy herself, Alan Jackson, Charlie Pride and some other stars would be invited and asked to sing a special carol. It was to be one of the most glittering, all-star shows that Music City had ever presented.

The news media in Nashville had been clamoring for a press conference with Susan, and she said okay after the show, but that it would have to be a short one. The Nashville papers—*The Banner* and *Tennessean*, TV and Radio stations were there.

"Just tell me your name, and who you represent," Susan requested. "This is the first press conference I've ever been to." The local and regional members of the press all knew Susan and had a deep affection for her.

One man present, a florid, sneering man, suddenly

asked roughly, "Is there a red hot romance going between you and Bradford?"

Susan's eyes turned cold and she demanded icily, "Who are you and who do you work for, you slimy toad?"

"My name don't matter, but I represent the *National Star Journal.*" It was one of the sleazy tabloids which dealt only in trash and dirt.

Susan pierced the man with her eyes, which seemed to be blazing with fury. She held nothing back and said directly to the man, "I don't use curse words, but I'm thinking them. Let's just say you are a dirty, rotten skunk and you know and everybody knows that Mr. Bradford and I are not having a romance. We are the closest of friends, and that's all. Now you get out of here, buster. I despise your kind." The man sneered again, but left.

Another member of the local news media, all of whom loved an respected Susan, put this question in, "Let's change the subject, Susan. Who do you think is the best female singer in country music?"

Susan grinned, "I sure wish I could claim it was me, but there's Reba, Dolly, Lorrie, Pam, Tammy, and so many others who are better than me, so that question is not hard to answer." Susan knew how to be diplomatic, paying her respects to her female competitors.

Susan put in an ad lib during the press conference, "I get awfully worried about the hate that's going on in this country. I love just about everybody, and I wish everybody would start thinking like that. You don't have to love everybody, but you sure don't have to be an enemy. One other important thing: Doug and I give to the Salvation Army in Boise to help feed hungry kids. A lot more people should be doing this in their hometowns."

After a few more friendly questions, Susan waved, said thanks and "see you in December."

Heading back west, we had time in Chicago for a sandwich and glass of milk, so soon after leaving O'Hare,

Susan got comfortable with a couple of pillows and snoozed like a beautiful doll.

I followed suit, just dozing for the most part, and somehow my thoughts again strayed way back in time. I thought to myself rather disgustedly, this is either my second or third childhood I'm going through. In junior high school I played the clarinet and saxophone in the band. We won some sort of city competition and our group was selected to appear with the great John Philip Sousa himself, who would direct us in one of his own marches. We practiced for several weeks on "The Thunderer." The Sousa band concert was at the Bijou Theater, which is apparently undergoing a face lift and many improvements including installing air conditioning.

Anyway, the time arrived and Mr. Sousa rapped his baton against his music stand and we played, I thought, very well. Mr. Sousa was flattering, too. Sometimes I wonder if any of the members of that junior high band are still alive.

I thought with deep pride of the document hanging on a bedroom wall. It is the original Civil War discharge from the U.S. Army of my grandfather, John A. Bradford, and is dated April 27, 1865, at Nashville, and said John Bradford was 18 years old when discharged. That meant he enlisted when he was 15. I had folks on both sides of the war, but Granddad John fought for the North. His discharge, slightly yellowed with age, is a real treasure for me.

Another time, I think in 1948, I was officially an academic doctor for half a day. The University of Utah in Salt Lake City was celebrating its 75th birthday, to my recollection, and scholars were invited from all over the world to attend. I didn't get a degree from the University of Tennessee, but was the closest ex-student, so I was asked to represent U-T, a tremendous honor.

Tennessee was the first land grant college in the young United States, the year being 1796, so I found

45

myself among the first ten men in line in the academic procession. I was sort of puffed up with my temporary importance, and tried to look dignified in my cap and gown. A rather short man was No. 1, and I don't remember which of the world's universities he represented, but he came along the line introducing himself. He got to me and I shook hands and said I was Douglas Bradford, Tennessee. The poor guy thought I said Doctor Bradford, so I was introduced that way to the other scholars, and that is how I was doctor for a day. An amusing but prideful moment in life.

* * * * *

We landed safely back in Boise, went to Susan's home, and Eric had two bottles of Heineken's ready for consumption. Thus ended Susan's third trip to Music City Tonight.

THE UGLY AND THE FUNNY

A couple of happenings occurred that week in Boise, one ugly and grim, the other hilarious. The ugly first.

Susan's one and only video was a top seller, and we got more dividends which were quite generous. So, I got sued for $500,000 by a young woman who claimed I had raped her and fathered her child. This is what happened.

At home one night about nine thirty, the phone rang and the caller said she was from the local paper and what was my reaction to a lawsuit which had been filed against me?

I told the reporter she must have the wrong number, that I knew of no suit against me. She pressed on, saying her paper had obtained a copy of the charges, and that I was accused of raping a nineteen-year-old girl and getting her pregnant. Again, I said I didn't know what she was talking about. I knew the next morning, for there was a spread on the front page which announced I indeed had been sued by a Miss Lowery, who wanted $500,000 as the aftermath of being raped and having my baby.

I swore special curses, and at eight that same morning, I called the judge's office which had issued the papers, and just then there was a knock, and a deputy sheriff or somebody from the court handed me the paper. I told the judge I was one mad citizen at being treated in such a manner, and I demanded an immediate trial. The judge apologized and seemed sincere, and said he could hold the trial the next morning at ten.

At Susan's house, her mother, Gloria, read the story first, and when Susan got up, she pointed out the story to her. Susan flared angrily and snapped, "He didn't do it and I'll bet he will call soon."

Sure enough, I did call and I told her the accusation was a lie, that it was plainly a blackmail and extortion attempt, and I hoped she could be at the trial the next morning.

So the next morning, the judge called the case of Anna Lowery, plaintiff, against Douglas Bradford, defendant.

Miss Lowery's attorney was named Augustus Fulbric, who had a very shady reputation. I asked the judge for the right to represent myself.

"Call your witness, Mr. Fulbric," the judge ordered.

Anna Lowery was quite a nice looking blond, who took the stand and was sworn in.

"What happened on the morning of July 30, 1993, Miss Lowery," her lawyer asked. "Just tell it in your own words."

She spoke slowly at first, saying she had let a man in her apartment who had asked to use the phone to call a service station to come and fix a flat tire. Then Anna's voice became more strident, and rushed through her story, saying the man had come in, and then turned and locked her door, and ordered her to take her clothes off. He said he was doing to do it to me (she used the "f" word) and I had better not make any noise or he would gag me.

"He looked mean, so I did take my clothes off, and then he made me watch him undress. I was scared at his nakedness and I knew he was going to hurt me. When he was done, he got up and dressed and threatened to beat up on me. Then he left."

Her lawyer asked, "Would you know this man if you saw him, and do you see him now?"

Anna turned dramatically and pointed to me and cried, "That's him. That's the man." Fulbric turned rather insolently to me and said, "Your witness."

I got up slowly and asked to be worn in, a surprise to the court and Fulbric.

Then I addressed Miss Lowery, "You know, you are under oath and you swore to tell the truth."

"I did tell the truth," she snapped back.

I saw Susan and her mother in the back of the courtroom, and a reporter from the local paper which had me smeared on their front page. I talked directly to the judge.

"Your honor, this is nothing more than a brazen attempt at blackmail and extortion. I want to introduce two documents as evidence. One paper is from my urologist doctor, and it is notarized, showing that he performed prostate cancer surgery on me on March 14, 1991. The other is from St. Luke's Hospital, attesting that the surgery was done there and that I was a patient in the hospital March 14–20, 1991.

"It is an unquestioned medical fact that when a man has his prostate removed, he no longer can get an erection. It is also an unquestioned fact that when his prostate is removed, he cannot produce the sperm which causes pregnancy in a woman. It is a plain fact that this young women has been lying. Her baby was born more than two years after my surgery, so there is no way I could be responsible for getting her pregnant. In a moment, I will ask for immediate dismissal of the blackmail, but I want to ask Miss Lowery a question or two.

"Do you still accuse me of being the man who raped you?"

She started sobbing. "I thought it was you," she cried.

"How did you get hooked up with this lawyer?" I queried.

She was sobbing. "A friend told me to go see him, that he could get me some easy money, and I was desperate, so I want to see him."

"How come it was me you decided on?" I asked

She answered haltingly. "He was reading the paper when I got there. I told him my troubles, and how bad I needed some money. He was reading a story about you and that girl singer making a lot of money, so he just pointed to your name and told me he would get $500,000 from you and you would pay it to keep from being embarrassed."

"How much was he going to give you?" I asked.

"Oh, he would give me $150,000, and that would get me out of a deep hole," she replied.

"But that would be only thirty percent for you, and he would take seventy percent, or $350,000," I pointed out. Miss Lowery said the attorney explained there would be heavy expenses, and the settlement would be fair to her.

I went on relentlessly, "So you and your lawyer just concocted this story, he made you rehearse it, and you were sure you were going to get a lot of money from me?"

She started sobbing again. "I just needed the money."

"Your honor," I addressed the judge, "I respectfully recommend to the court that it in turn recommend to the Ada County Bar Association and the Idaho State Bar Association that this man who claims to be an attorney, that he be disbarred from practicing law in Idaho. He is one of the reasons that lawyers have gotten a tarnished reputation.

"Now, Judge, I ask for an immediate dismissal of these charges."

"So ordered," His Honor declared.

With the case closed, I joined Susan and Gloria and we stopped for coffee on the way home.

Glad to report that that two-bit shyster was indeed kicked out of the legal profession and he no longer can practice law in Idaho.

THE DEVIL MADE ME DO IT

The happy story:

By this time in October 1994, Susan had appeared on Music City Tonight three times, and had become one of the best-known young women in Boise. She was highly popular, and got numerous invitations from all sides to attend various functions. She was gracious in turning them down, pointing out that she was too busy with her school work. I was generally invited too, but when I wasn't, Susan insisted I go along.

A surprising change took place in mid-month. I received two gold engraved invitations to an afternoon tea, and from no less a prominent source than Mrs. Montegu Dusenberry,, who liked to be thought of as the real lioness of Boise society, but was called Mrs. Doozyberry by some unimpressed people.

The invitation said for me and guest, so I told Susan this was a must, she *must* go with me. I chuckled when I explained, "She's a mean, ornery old bitch, both snooty and snotty. We ought to have a rip roarin' time."

I called the mandatory acceptance, leaving word that my companion and I would have to leave early.

My '94 Grand Am looked rather dilapidated when we rolled up the driveway, loaded with Caddies, Continentals, a BMW, and a Mercedes.

We walked to the door, to be greeted by Mrs. Doozy herself, who almost recoiled when she noticed Susan, who was probably the first black person ever to be a guest in this elegant mansion.

We took our seats, accepted a glass of weak punch, and Susan smiled at most of the people who recognized her.

Mrs. Doozy marched into the room, with a huge Great Dane tagging along. The dog started sniffing the feet of the guests, stopped in front of me, expelled some malodorous gas, and I drew back from the odor.

Mrs. D rushed to me seat and asked if Winston, her dog, had been offensive.

The devil made me say, rather loudly, "Naw, he just farted in my face." I heard several gasps from the women, and Mrs. Doozy recoiled several feet. I sat innocently as if nothing impolite had been said. An old-timer dressed in ranch clothes winked, and I had a hard time to keep from doubling over with laughter.

We took leave shortly thereafter, thanking Mrs. D. profusely for her hospitality, and said we hoped to be invited again. The look on the old bag's face said that was not likely.

The minute we got out of the door, Susan went on a giggling spree as we walked to the car.

Susan commented gravely, "You know, Mr. B, I sort of doubt if we're going to get invited back. Anyway, I hope not. You were right, she's a rotten, spoiled old goat."

As for me, I felt uplifted inside, having insulted the old bitch in her own home.

A SONG AND A POEM

Later, one evening in October, I called to take Susan out to dinner, and she was still primping a little bit, so Eric suggested calling on Dr. Heineken for some of his medicine. I accepted gladly, and was nursing a second bottle when Susan came in, looking glamorous as usual. I admired her openly and commented, "Miss Susan, Ah reckon Ah'm feelin' kind of flirty tonight. Can I flirt with you, ma'am?"

Susan beamed, "Podnah, you all can flirt with me anytime you like."

I answered sort of bashfully, "Better brace yourself because I finally got the nerve to sing you a little song." It must be pointed out that any resemblance to my voice and singing a tune is purely coincidental. But I gave it a try, sitting at the piano and using only one hand.

TO SUSAN

I want to sing and shout, tell all the world about
A little gal named Susan;
I want to squeeze her so, and never let her go,
That's what I think about Susan:
Oh, those big brown eyes, and pretty curls,
Oh, you're my choice, of all the girls.
Your dimpled smile is such a treat
And everybody knows that you're so sweet,
I want to sing and shout, tell all the world about,
A little gal named Susan.

Susan was delighted and wanted to know if I had written the song for her. I had to tell her no, it was written about twenty-five years ago for my first granddaughter, but she never heard it and nobody else has heard it except you, so it is your song. I was rewarded with a big hug.

"I ain't finished yet, sweetie. I got a poem to read to you. And this one was written just for you."

> I love you daily, I love you nightly,
> I love you very, very mightily;
> You light up my life, you light up my world,
> Look into my heart, there's love unfurled;
> Let's blend into one, just you and me,
> Our love for each other will make history;
> Together we'll fly to Cloud Number Nine,
> I will be yours, and you will be mine;
> Gotta be that way, nothing else will do,
> I'll start each day and say I love you;
> You spread the joy wherever you are,
> You create sunshine both wide and far.

Eric, Gloria, and Sally all exclaimed that was one of the prettiest poems they ever heard. Susan threw out her chest and declaimed, "I've had a song and poem written about me all in one day."

She continued without missing a beat, "Now, Podnah, where are you taking me to dinner?"

I suggested a Big Mac, and she snorted, and said come on, she will tell me which way to go. The bossier she was, the cuter she became, and I thanked my lucky stars for the thousandth time at being so close to such a charming young lady.

P.S. We did not get a Big Mac.

A VISIT FROM SUSAN

I was sitting at my kitchen table one morning with a stack of papers scattered around when I heard the throaty purr of a car out front, and in a moment Susan was rapping at the front door. She came in and immediately started fanning the air, waving her hands as if the whole house was on fire. She scowled and spoke her usual piece—I was smoking too much.

I commented complacently, "Now that the lecture is done, what brings you to my humble shack on this beautiful day?"

"You haven't called in a week," she complained. "You trying to get rid of me?"

"Madam," I replied gallantly, "I would not think of trying to lose the most beautiful girl in the world with the most beautiful voice in the whole dang-blasted world."

She sniffed, and asked what was I doing with all those papers? I explained that I was trying to fine tune three great story lines for Bob Hope TV specials.

"Mr. Hope needs new material to get him sparkling again, and if he is interested in doing anymore TV specials, I modestly claim these are three major league ideas."

She gave orders for me to go to my TV reading chair, smoke a cigarette, while she inspected the Bob Hope material.

I kid you not. They are three captivating story lines.

One is "Road to the Golf Course," starring Bob and George Burns, plus Brooke Shields, Bill Cosby and a cameo by Hulk Hogan. In this story, Bob is determined to become the king and czar of all golfdom, and is buying up all the golf courses in the country.

The hilarious ending, after an adventurous cross-country tour, has George dropping a bombshell. George says that he himself has been buying all the 19th holes while Bob was acquiring only the courses themselves. George added, with rather a sadistic pleasure, that the 19th holes was where all the money was. Bob is devastated and gives an Oscar performance with his grief and sorrow and bitter disappointment. But there's a happy ending.

(George Burns died at the age of 100 after this was written, and the whole world seemed deeply saddened.)

The second story is entitled "Road to Mount Rushmore." Margaret Thatcher gave a speech in this country and she recommended that Bob's image be placed at Mount Rushmore alongside the four great presidents. The former British Prime Minister pointed out that everybody knew that Bob was born in England, and the colonies would make the mother country happy if it honored Bob. Bob agonized over the matter, whether he deserved such a high honor or not, and finally friend and former President Ronald Reagan came up with a happy solution.

The last story was "Road to Carnegie Hall," in which Bob takes a group of sixteen highly-talented youngsters on a cross country trip, with stops in Chicago, Cleveland, Philadelphia, Knoxville, and other major cities, winding up at Carnegie Hall two nights before Christmas. The kids were sensational successes wherever they performed, and Bob had promised to get them home for Christmas Eve. Their home flight from New York found their plane caught in a fierce blizzard in the Rocky Mountains and they had to land in a remote area of Utah. The strip was little used except in warmer months, but with a good-sized building available. They lost communications, but finally got the plane's radio going, were bussed to Salt Lake City behind a snow plow, and reached the Burbank airport just as Christmas eve was starting.

Susan appeared in a daze, but was impressed. "These are excellent. Have you gotten them to Mr. Hope yet?" she asked.

I told her I had tried, but there were several layers of assistants, lawyers, and others below Bob and I was given word that Mr. Hope never considered unsolicited material. So the chances are very remote that Bob will ever get to hear these ideas. He could use them.

Anyway, Susan let me smoke another cigarette, and then we had a leisurely lunch.

AHOY, NASHVILLE: CHRISTMAS AND SUSAN ARE ON THE WAY

November and Thanksgiving went by leisurely, and it was time to head for Nashville, and Susan's fourth appearance in 1994 on Music City Tonight.

No trouble in Chicago, but after about thirty minutes en route south to Nashville, the captain came on the speaker to announce, "Folks, we just got a report from our weather station, and there is a blizzard developing that will cover much of the south, east, and midwest. We will get to Nashville in plenty of time, there is no need to worry."

Susan muttered, "Thank goodness, let's get on the ground." We did, and shortly after limousining to the Opryland Hotel, the blizzard hit with an untamed fury. Outside was nothing but thick, blowing snow, and visibility was about zero. We were thankful to be inside, warm and comfortable. The dinner was excellent, as usual, especially after a shot of Dr. Heineken's medicine. After dinner, a lengthy stroll in the hotel, which seemed to grow in beauty and with the towering Christmas tree with thousands and thousands of shiny lights.

I had arranged for two rooms with a connecting door, and Susan was not at all worried. She could keep her side of the door locked, and if she needed me, just had to knock.

Next morning another luscious breakfast with those

wonderful, tasty delicacies—ham and eggs and red eye gravy and hot biscuits and honey. Outside, the blizzard continued to rage, and two or three feet of snow accumulated. A little worry started buzzing in my head, but sloshily we made it to the adjacent Gaslight Theater. We found Jim Owens with a scowl on his face and a concerned look. Buddy Skipper, Wanda, and drummer Bobby were there, still kicking snow from their boots.

Jim Owens got our attention. "Lorianne was going to try to get here this morning, but I gave her strict orders not to try it, so she won't be here. Reba is stranded in Oklahoma, Alan Jackson in Pittsburgh, and the rest of the band can't make it. Charlie is still in California on special assignment, so it looks like we'll have to cancel the big Christmas show tonight and use a re-run. Dang it, this was going to be the best show of the year. Reckon you can't argue with the weatherman, so you all will just have to dig in and find something to do."

That's when Five Star General Susan Sanders took over. She rose to her full five foot three inch height, and with more than a little indignation in her voice, notified Jim Owens with this broadside:

"Mr. Owens, what do you mean we have to cancel? We've got a lot of talent here. You got Buddy Skipper, and Wanda, and Bobby, and little old me. Doug could fill in some spots. We can put a show on and I think all of us want to try it."

Jim looked at Susan fondly, and advised, "Young lady, you got guts, but we're too short-handed to put on a ninety minute program."

Wanda chimed in. This usually reserved young lady now spoke firmly and advised right back, "Mr. Owens, we've got enough talent to put on a show."

Susan made this addition, and there was some steel creeping in her voice. "I thought there was an old saying that the show had to go on. Well, let's go on. We have until five o'clock to make plans, so why don't we get busy."

To Jim Owens' credit, he knew determination when he saw it. He broke out in a big grin, and said this, "What is everybody waiting for. Let's get busy. We'll go for it, and have a lot of fun. There's loads of talent, and maybe Doug will have some ideas."

My nervous stomach launched an attack right about then, but I managed to convey the thought that I had a few corny jokes I could tell. So, by gosh, we all went to work. A brief break for a sandwich at noon, and by three thirty we had the outline of a pretty good show, but one that would put tremendous pressure on the four star entertainers.

We knocked off at four fifteen, mentally if not physically exhausted, and I gratefully lit a cigarette in the no smoking zone. We relaxed for five minutes, then Jim said there were some clothes in wardrobe that would fit all of us, and to get dressed up.

We started to the dressing rooms, and Jim said casually to Susan and me, "By the way, Mr. Bradford, you and Miss Sanders will co-host the show."

I gulped, felt like swooning, and tried to stay calm outwardly. Susan, that precious young woman of steel, appeared radiant, and exclaimed happily, "Wow. Sure, me and Doug can do it." I wanted to hug her, so maybe she could hold me up and keep me from falling, but I stumbled into the dressing room. We all got a decent set of outfits, very casual, to make us feel more comfortable.

The clock was winding down, and at exactly five, here came a sub announcer's voice, "Welcome to Music City Tonight, with special co-hosts, Miss Susan Sanders and Mr. Douglas Bradford. You're going to see a show tonight that you will never forget, brought to you by a group of brave entertainers who beat the blizzard. They are stubborn examples of the old saying 'The Show Must Go On.'"

Susan and I ducked out of our dressing rooms, she taking my arm as we proceeded out to the stage. Thankfully, I remembered to bow to Buddy Skipper, and he cocked his hand like a pistol and bowed back.

THE SHOW STARTS

That firm grasp on my arm somehow sent a surge of confidence through me, and we took center stage and greeted the crowd, although we couldn't see how many were in the audience until our eyes got adjusted to the bright lights.

I opened up hesitantly. "Welcome to Music City Tonight, folks. We're a little short on manpower, but there's plenty of quality entertainment." By then, I could see how skimpy the crowd was. "Hey, you folks out there," I greeted, "thanks for being here. I hope you are here to see the show and not just that you ducked in from the blizzard to get out of the cold."

Lo and behold, I started to feel a little comfortable, and Susan broke in with this, "Folks, I wish we could say we had an all-star lineup tonight, but that dang-blasted weatherman has tried to spoil our party. But we're gonna have some Christmas carols, and you all can join in, and we will sure keep the Christmas spirit alive. Now, Mr. B, what is the opening number?"

I couldn't help grinning. Susan had everything under control, so I just announced: "A famous number that everybody knows. Susan and the entire band of three members will give us 'When the Saints Come Marching In.'"

Susan commanded the piano to sit up and start to work. Buddy Skipper had his clarinet going at full steam.

Wanda made her fiddle wake up joyously, and there were some peppy drum beats from Bobby.

First number—A-Okay!

I looked out at the crowd, saw how sparse it was, and made a request. "You all are too scattered out. Would you all mind moving up and filling the first few rows? We've got to be one big happy family. When you get all bunched up, would you count off just to see how many brave souls are here?" They counted, and there were exactly 101 men and women and a few children in the 600-seat auditorium.

"Folks, I salute you for being here. I hope this will be a show you can tell the grandkids about. Now, here's more music. Buddy and Wanda will give you 'Limehouse Blues.'"

Again, smooth sailing, and we got the signal from the booth that it was time for a commercial. Kelly Springfield, America's oldest tire company, presented its message.

I told the folks they would have to put up with a couple of stories from me, so the professionals could take a brief rest.

I started out by declaring how much we all missed Lorianne and Charlie, and that we were pretty poor substitutes, but we would do our best.

I commenced, "You don't have to bust a gut from laughing at my stories, but I sure hope you'll be a little polite and try a couple of chuckles. If Lorianne was here, she'd whack me on the arm for this first story, but it not dirty and not even naughty.

"One time a grandmother took her little five-year-old granddaughter shopping, and grandma saw a sweater with a deep v-neck she said she was going to buy for herself. But the granddaughter immediately objected, 'Oh, no grandma, you mustn't get a sweater like this. Mother got one last week just like that one, and every time she bends over, her lungs fall out.'"

The crowd howled and applauded, and I took a polite bow, and even got a couple of drum rolls from Bobby.

I couldn't help grinning, and told the audience, "I'm sure Lorianne is watching and hope she didn't blush at that story. Let me tell you something. A few years ago, Minnie Pearl had a segment on Ralph Emery's Nashville Now show, and she would read three jokes which had been sent in. Minnie read this one one night, and was laughing so hard she could barely get through it. Of course, it was the big winner. So Lorianne, if Minnie Pearl would tell it, then I could steal it from Minnie and tell it, too. And Minnie Pearl, you are the No. 1 All American Girl. I happen to be one of at least 50 million men who love you and we all send our love tonight. I may have to call on you to defend me from Lorianne."

(Minnie Pearl, the lovable country music legend, passed away shortly after this was written. Millions of country music fans mourned her passing.)

I tried another quick one. "Most of you remember Bum Phillips, the former National Football League coach. Bum retired several years ago, and a friend asked what he was doing in his retirement. Bum just replied, 'I ain't doing a damn thing, and I don't start until noon.'"

That was the best one liner of the year, and got some chuckles.

Then it was time for the main feature. I got serious again. Susan spoke softly into the mike and offered, "I'd like to sing everybody's favorite Christmas carol, 'Silent Night.'"

She started tenderly, with Wanda blending in perfectly with the harmony, and then her voice soared into the heavens. She was compelling, brilliant, and magnificent. As the last words of the song faded into the stillness "sleep in heavenly peace," everybody there and everybody all over the country realized that Susan indeed had sung like an angel. The crowd of 101 rose to its feet, and applauded like 10,000. I swear I thought at the moment that God Himself had listened and joined in the applause.

All I could think of to do was bow almost reverently to Susan, and she knew the love and respect in that bow. I said to the crowd, "That memorable song by Susan made this a real Christmas show."

Sixty minutes of our ninety minute show had passed, and we knew that so far we had done pretty good.

I tried a couple more stories, and the crowd loosened up on the first one. The second one got a few snickers.

The first one was about a rough and tough construction man, whose only passion was to get the job done on time. "Get the job done, put more men on the job," he would yell. "Get it done and put more men on the job."

His wife and five-year-old daughter knew of his two commands. Christmas was near, and this rough and tough boss asked his daughter what she wanted Santa Claus to bring her. "Oh, Daddy, I want a little brother," she exclaimed. The boss man shook his head and informed his daughter, "Sorry, sweetie, there just isn't enough time."

The daughter was trifle indignant. "Daddy, can't you put more men on the job?"

The chuckles were appreciated, but the next one got some loud silence:

"A woman died and went to Heaven. St. Peter met her at the Golden Gates and asked, 'What is God's first name? Do you know it?'

"The woman said, 'Sure, It's Andy.'

"St. Peter was puzzled and asked why she thought that.

"The woman replied simply, 'God's name is in that beautiful hymn we sing—'Andy walks with me, Andy talks with me, Andy tells me I am his own.'"

A few polite hand claps was all that resulted.

Back to another major feature. I proudly announced

that Susan's next song would be the one that made her famous—"Home in Tennessee."

With Wanda providing the harmony, Susan gave the song new meaning, the notes coming from her heart. She bowed gracefully at the end, and again the 101 thundered their appreciation.

Susan and Buddy and Wanda and Bobby played and the crowd sang several Christmas carols, and there was a real yuletide spirit that could be felt.

I told the crowd that I had one more story to tell, and there were some groans. But they heard this:

"A drunk staggered into the Salvation Army soup kitchen one night, and said he needed something to eat. The commander thought a moment, and said the drunk could have a meal if he could tell a story from the Bible. The drunk pondered, and then his face lit up, and he said he would tell about that guy Simpson, who took the jawbone of a mule and beat the ass off 10,000 Filipinos."

Finally, I got a huge reaction, and the crowd gave me a nice bunch of hand claps. I bowed to the 101 in appreciation.

I called Buddy, Wanda, Bobby, and Susan to center stage, and told the crowd, "Folks, meet some real heroes." The slim crowd roared its appreciation, and the four heroes took keep bows.

Me again: "Folks, that is our show for tonight. You are all heroes, too, but please drive carefully when you leave, because those roads and streets are treacherous. Lorianne will be here tomorrow night, so tune in. God bless every one of you, and good night from Music City Tonight!"

ONE TIRED GAL

We were off the air, and Susan sank wearily onto the couch, utterly exhausted. She had been delivering at least two dozen tunes on her piano, and looked quite pitiful. She mourned, "Podnah, I'm a tired gal. I'm plumb tuckered out."

Buddy, Wanda, and Bobby also looked beat. I felt like it, too, but they had done all the work.

Jim Owens came in and went to Susan and did a deep bow. "Susan," he started, "you were wonderful, and so were the rest of you. This is Susan's fourth time on the show, and you have become a major star. I'll bet we get hundreds of calls and cards and letters giving all of you a pat on the back, and you sure deserve it."

Jim continued, "This show was nothing but plain old guts and determination, and you all were outstanding. I didn't think you could do it, but you sure did. Goshamighty, I'm glad you two gals talked me into it, because I was ready to chicken out. This show will be talked about for a long, long time. You two young women must have show blood in your veins, and I'll bet a million to one that everybody watching enjoyed every minute of it, even those lousy stories that Doug told."

I leaned back in my chair and smiled, very happy inside and out.

Jim again, "There will be generous bonuses for all of you for performing way beyond the call of duty. I'd like you to know how deeply your talents are appreciated."

Then Jim turned to us and said firmly, "Oh yes, Miss Sanders and Mr. Bradford, you did so good I'd like you to stay over and co-host the show tomorrow night with Lorianne."

I told Jim it was impossible because Susan was so worn out she couldn't do another ninety minute show.

Jim was insistent. "Susan won't have to do anything

except sit next to Lorianne. We are certainly going to have a re-run of "Silent Night," and Susan can sit and hear herself sing. If she feels like doing another song, that would be extra nice," he added.

I started to refuse again, but Susan nudged me and decided we would stay over. She commented simply: "If I get a good night's sleep, and maybe a short nap in the afternoon, I'll be okay."

I gave in grudgingly, because even though she has a lot of steel in her spine, she also is on the fragile side.

I asked what honorarium Susan would get, and Jim said $5,000 would be suitable. I frowned a bit and said $7,500 would sound better, and Jim grinned and said okay.

So Susan had a bowl of soup and I helped her to her room. I stepped into my own room while she got into her pajamas, then went in and tucked her in bed and gave her a kiss on the forehead. I told her I would have a Heineken's, eat a bite, take a walk, and be back around nine o'clock. She murmured all right and was soon sound asleep and breathing evenly.

I had my beer, a decent meal, short walk, and got back to my room at nine. I got into my own pajamas and was just climbing into bed, when there came a knock on the connecting door. Susan opened it a crack and said rather plaintively, "I gotto have a hug. I'm your granddaughter, I had a rough day and need a little tender loving care." She got her hug, smiled tiredly but happily, closed the door and returned to her bed.

I was up at six and Susan was still sleeping soundly. I showered and shaved, went down for some breakfast and returned about eight thirty.

I knocked on her door, went in and shook her gently.

"Wanna get up?" I asked. She opened her eyes slowly, then yawned and stretched and grumbled: "Naw, I don't want to get up but I reckon I will. I feel a lot better and if you'll get me something to eat, I'll be ready to go."

While she bathed, I went to the coffee shop and got her a big glass of orange juice, some hot rolls and honey and butter.

She ate with real satisfaction, and said she would try to go all day.

We went down to the Gaslight Theater at ten, and the minute we walked on stage, Lorianne dashed up and gave Susan a tremendous hug. She spoke with love in her voice. "Susan, I cried last night when you sang so wonderfully. It was the most beautiful voice I have ever heard and Jim tells me we will re-run 'Silent Night' tonight. You were simply marvelous, and I'm so glad you and Doug will co-host with me tonight."

"Reba will be here, and so will Alan. I got Charlie Pride and he is in town and will join us, and they will all sing a Christmas carol, so we will have our second Christmas show tonight."

Rehearsals were held, but with that group of stars, they didn't need much practice. We had a brief lunch break, and Susan was listless and obviously still on the worn side. I told Lorianne and Jim that Susan might not last the whole ninety minutes, but she got an hour's nap in the afternoon, and insisted on heading for the dressing room to get dolled up for the show.

The time passed rather quickly. Reba was outstanding as usual, Alan Jackson was at his best, and that likeable Charlie Pride was tremendous. Susan felt well enough and did a lively "It's Beginning to Look a Lot Like Christmas."

Ten minutes before the close, Lorianne told the packed house of 600 that last night everybody heard the unforgettable voice of Susan Sanders singing "Silent Night." "We'll play the re-run tonight, and see if you agree with me that it was never been sung as beautiful."

The audience had gotten word of the beauty of the song, and there was total stillness as Susan's magical voice sang "Silent Night" again. The crowd gave Susan a standing ovation, and she bowed gracefully. We were soon off the air.

Susan managed to stand and say our goodbyes, but literally collapsed onto the couch. I ordered the house doctor to come quick. Lorianne helped Susan to her room and into her night clothes. The doctor gave a frank opinion that Susan was thoroughly exhausted, both physically and mentally, and should stay in bed for two or three days. Susan was alert enough to respond rather tartly, "We're going home tomorrow, and tomorrow night I'll be in my own bed, and that will make me feel better very quick." The doc was dubious, and said the plane trip would be an ordeal, but gave Susan some pills to take that would help on the trip home. Then he left.

Lorianne tucked Susan into bed, and she also left, asking that we call the next night to let her know how Susan felt. Lorianne said good night, glancing back with a worried look on her face.

Susan was already sound asleep as I closed the connecting door and got wearily into my own bed.

BACK TO BOISE AGAIN

Our return trip the next day was much better than expected. Opryland Hotel and United joined together to make Susan's trip as comfortable as possible. The limo took us to the airport, a go-cart took Susan to our departure gate, and she was wheeled into our first-class seats to settle down among several pillows. Susan had orange juice and a small roll and glass of milk en route to Chicago, then slept most of the way to Boise. Her folks met us at the airport, and Susan insisted I come by their house for awhile. I did, but stayed only a few minutes, telling them that the old man was whupped down and heading for the sack. I told Susan to sleep until noon, and I would call to see how she was feeling. If she felt up to it, we'd get a bite of lunch somewhere. In front of her folks, Susan gave me a big hug and kiss, and I knew there was deep, tender love between us.

I was in bed by nine, up at six, wobbled to the kitchen to put the coffee on, wobbled to the front door for the morning paper, then retired with the sports page to the proper reading surroundings.

I had my usual three cups, but a worry was nagging at me, and I knew it was Susan's health.

This twenty-year-old marvel had enormous stamina, but even her staying power had to stretch out thin sometimes, as in Nashville for two hectic nights. I worried about her heart, her lungs, her blood pressure, her vocal chords, her stress limit. I decided that only a complete and thorough physical exam would give some reassurance that her health was not in jeopardy.

I called her at eleven thirty, and she was up and drinking coffee, and why didn't I come to see her. I stopped at Delsa's and got her favorite chocolate ice cream. She was plumb tickled and ate most of it.

Then I told her and her mother, Gloria, that a complete physical was absolutely necessary, and I wanted the opinions of the top specialists in Boise.

Susan objected, of course, saying she would be fine in a day or two. I told her this, "My little turtle dove, I'm the boss on this, and we're going to make sure there is nothing wrong with you." Gloria agreed, so we made appointments with the best medical people in town. Susan was scheduled for that complete physical in ten days, by both male and female doctors.

Susan got a thorough going over, and instead of relieving all of us, it only added to the worry. The leading eye, ear, and throat specialist was puzzled by some trouble he detected in Susan's throat. It could be a variant of strep throat, he advised, and he told Susan she should not sing one note for at least thirty days.

Another doctor who specialized in stress situations mentioned that Susan's own stressful life in Nashville he said could be related to what he called ARDS, which I believe he explained meant Adult Respiratory Distress Syndrome. He told Susan straightforward that she should try to keep out of any stress situations, and warned that development in this problem could be dangerous. Susan listened and I believe she was convinced that she had to take better care of herself.

Susan did obey her orders pretty good, but thirty days later, when she returned to the throat specialist, the doc said frankly he could not pinpoint any signs of permanent damage to her health.

All of us continued to worry.

During our day in Nashville in December, Lorianne had invited Susan to sing again in February, but Susan declined saying she was focusing on graduating in late spring. An early date in May was agreed upon, because by then, Susan said, she would have her studies under control.

SUSAN AND SALLY

With Susan apparently feeling much better, we planned to go out to dinner and I called for her about seven.

Sally opened the door, saying Susan was still primping and would I come in and meet a friend of hers.

Her friend was a handsome young black man whose name was Richard Sawyer. He was tall, with a muscular build and looked a great deal like Jubilant Sykes, and I wondered how I came up with that name.

Sally said rather slyly that she and Richard had a song they were working on, and would I listen because Richard had a powerful baritone voice.

Sally parked at the piano, and then she and her friend did a splendid version of "Only Make Believe," from the Jerome Kern classic that featured Old Man River in Showboat.

Sally did the high parts and harmony, and when they finished, I applauded vigorously, it was so well done. Susan had slipped in the room and also clapped.

"Richard," I said, "you've got the makings, and Sally, I've always known you had great talent. You make a wonderful team. Richard, do you bust a gut practicing each day?"

He answered seriously, "Mr. Bradford, I bust a gut about a hundred times a week. I'm majoring in music like Sally, and when I met her and heard her sing, I knew we would be a team."

"If both of you keep at it and keep improving, Susan and I would try to take you to Nashville and let some important people hear you sing. Sally, you are weak on your high notes, and you know it, so work on your power."

Sally grinned, and said she would, because that is what her teacher told her.

"Sally," I complimented, "you were a first-class brat a year ago. You sure have matured and I am very proud of you." She beamed in appreciation.

Susan and I commented pleasantly about Sally and Richard over dinner. Susan gave a wry grin and said she thought Sally was falling in love with one man instead of two dozen.

Susan concentrated on her studies, and followed the doctor's orders, resting her throat for a full month before she tried singing again. Her voice was regaining its old magic, so we planned for her May date in Nashville.

I had written a lively song called "I'm at the Halfway House to Heaven, I'm Gonna Go All the Way," which Susan liked and learned quickly. For her other number I suggested an old, old favorite that probably nobody remembered, "The Barefoot Trail" about a boy with a freckled nose and a lassie lovely as a rose. Again, Susan loved it and had it down pat. She did a rousing San Antonio Rose in between, honoring her hometown.

So, to Nashville the first week of May, and it was one of the most interesting of all the trips.

Goodness Always Stronger Than Badness

When the five o'clock taping started, Charlie was unusually serious, with no zingers for Lorianne that night. He candidly remarked that he was depressed, reading about racial gang troubles breaking out all over the country.

Susan was backstage and heard Charlie's comments. After her second number, which as usual got thunderous applause, Susan spoke some words that momentarily electrified the country.

"Charlie," she started slowly, "you're right. Those problems belong to all of us. This is probably a simple thought, but I wish all people everywhere would realize that there is some goodness, no matter how small, in all of us everywhere. That goodness is really there."

Susan asked poignantly, "Why are so many people mad at each other? Why can't people of all races—white, black, red, brown, and yellow—and those awful hate groups, just try for a little while to forget their prejudices. Let them all allow that goodness to break out inside themselves, and whip the badness, because goodness always is stronger than badness. Just think how much happier most people would be, and what a happier country we would have."

The crowd erupted spontaneously. Lorianne and Charlie shook their heads in admiration and amazement that a twenty-year-old African-American could express such a noble, dynamic idea in understandable words.

"What wonderful words to keep in mind," Charlie exclaimed. "What a beautiful way she has of outlining the path to a happier country. How I wish that people all over the country could hear those thoughts."

Lo and behold, Susan's simple thunderbolts did catch fire. Both Nashville newspapers—*The Banner* and *Tennessean*—gave front page coverage, plus ringing editorial endorsements, and the story spread nationwide. Governors joined in praise. The President, who never missed a chance to grab on to a popular idea, mentioned it in his weekly radio talk.

And Billy Graham, whom I consider to be the No. 1 citizen of the world, used *Goodness Is Always Stronger Than Badness* as the theme for a rousing sermon.

All of a sudden, Susan was famous nationwide. Congratulations poured in, and invitations to speak came from all over. We had to rent a large post office box back in Boise to handle the deluge of mail.

We also had to prepare a standard response, that Susan deeply appreciated their interest, but that she was head over heels with school work and getting ready to graduate from Boise State University. The responses were Xeroxed, but Susan signed each one personally.

She pointed out that each community had capable leaders who could nourish the idea in their hometowns. She was sent editorials from newspapers across the country, including a ponderous one from the *New York Times,* and a meaty writing from the *Washington Post.*

She asked the Associated Press to send out a story nationwide, thanking all the people for the thoughtfulness.

Thus, thanks to Susan Sanders of Boise, Idaho, there was a momentary gleam of hope in the soul of America. For a brief interval, all people did seem happier and goodness did prevail.

But badness tragically refused to surrender.

LORIANNE AND CHARLIE

A big disappointment happened at the May show. Lorianne and Charlie announced they were leaving Music City Tonight on next November 17, and would announce their new plans soon. Susan took the news hard, saying that Lorianne and Charlie were two of the brightest stars on television, and that Music City Tonight was the best program on the air. But Susan was invited to be on that November 17 final program, with other stars to be announced.

The trip back to Boise was routine. Nice lunch out of Chicago, then Susan curled up for a nap. I started living in the past again, recalling some amusing incidents.

I may have mentioned that I was administrative assistant to the governor of Idaho from 1967 to 1971. He was a robust man, and the fiercest guardian of the tax dollar of any governor before or since. With tax money, he was a tightwad.

When we moved into the governor's office, I noticed there were no reference books, and I asked the governor if we could buy a set of encyclopedias. He thought a moment, then said, "Sure, when they come out in paperback."

He invited all the Indian tribes to Boise each spring to offer them help from any state department or agency. I got well acquainted with a chief of the Kootenai tribe from North Idaho. His name was Ozzie, and one afternoon in a saloon, he told me the story of his great grandfather. "Grandfather was the greatest warrior in the history of the tribe," Ozzie related. "He had one small problem; he was a little goofy. He didn't know heads from tails, and he brought home some of the damnedest looking scalps."

I visited Sun Valley quite often. Once, in a crowded lobby at the Sun Valley Lodge, I accidentally bumped into a woman and she responded with "Gahdammit, dahling, watch where you're going." It was Norma Shearer. I had a beer with Gary Cooper in the Challenger Lounge, inviting him to come to Twin Falls as honorary referee for some Golden Gloves boxing matches. The affable Gary did come, and as always, everybody liked him.

I talked with Clark Gable on the telephone, inviting him to become a member of the Twin Falls American Legion Post. He said, "Sure, count me in." Tyrone Power was a first-class jerk, refusing to meet or have his picture taken with Miss Idaho American Legion queen.

About thirty minutes from Boise, the flight attendant came by, and seeing Susan curled up sleeping, offered, "Mr. Bradford, she looks like an angel." A sudden chill went through my body, and for some reason, those words were disturbing.

Towards the end of May, the phone rang one morning and a sweet voice caroled, "Mr. B, I hereby invite you to attend my graduation exercises next week at Boise State. You will sit with my folks." I had my orders and obeyed. The hundreds of grads paraded across the stage, getting their diplomas. The state Board of Education president announced "Miss Susan Sanders," and the Sanders family and I applauded loudly. Susan was now a college graduate.

The night called for a special celebration, for Susan's birthday came a few days later.

We decided on the elegant dining room at the Red Lion Riverside. When the meal was over, I took a small, neatly wrapped box from my pocket, handed it to Susan and just said "happy birthday." She cried when she opened it, and asked—rather ordered—me to turn over my handkerchief. The gift was quite nice, and rather expensive, a golden necklace with rubies entwined, and I told her she was now my golden girl. The hug and affection in her look were worth a million dollars.

The summer passed. Susan entered BSU in the fall to start work on her masters degree, but easily got permission to be absent November 16 and 17.

Lorianne called and asked Susan to sing her Tennessee song as one number, and to find something appropriate for the second number. I told Susan there was a beautiful old-time song called "End of a Perfect Day." We got the sheet music, Susan learned it, and it was a lovely melody and ideal for the closer.

MUSIC CITY TONIGHT BECOMES HISTORY

Lorianne and Charlie had announced last May they were leaving Music City Tonight, and the week of November 11 would be their final few days. The last show came on Friday night, November 17, and it was an all-star lineup, with Susan as one of the top stars. Lorianne explained that after November 17, re-runs of old MCT shows would run until January 15, and that she and Charlie would start a syndicated show January 29. She also told everybody present that there were to be no tears and no sadness for the final program.

(The Crook and Chase syndicated show has become highly popular and plays most markets throughout the country.)

I said all-stars, and it was true, for the November 17 special. Reba wished the two popular members of the team the best of luck, then Barbara Mandrell broke in to add her own best wishes.

Billy Ray Cyrus and Pam Tillis, both famous in their own right, sang, and the Jordanaires and Crownsmen furnished their musical talents.

The Music City band, with leader Buddy Skipper, plus singers, performed and drew sustained applause. I thought to myself these people were the best in the business.

Then Susan was announced, to sing her own famous Tennessee song, and she drew the most hand claps. Susan had been fascinated by the other stars, and she had a warm smile.

Susan gave her heart to her song, except on the final phase, which she usually sang with piercing high notes. She had some difficulty with her throat, and only I noticed it.

Billy Ray, the Crownsmen, and the Jordanaires performed the semi-final number, doing one of Billy Ray's hits, "One Night With You."

Then Susan was announced for the final number to be sung on Music City Tonight. She bowed to the crowd, took her place at the piano, and told the crowd she chose one of the most beautiful songs ever written, "End of a Perfect Day" as her choice.

"Perfect Day" had wondrous harmony, and Wanda was her usual skillful best, and the song faded away with Susan singing, "And the sun goes down with a flaming ray, and the dear friends have to part." Again, Susan skipped all the high notes.

Lorianne was brushing away the tears, and all there had lumps in their throats, but happy smiles soon broke out, and the show closed on a glorious note.

When we went off the air, Susan gripped my arm

tightly, and I helped her to the couch. She said huskily that her throat was sore, and she wanted to go to her room and lie down.

There were hugs and kisses and handshakes. I heard Lorianne whisper to Susan that she was the best thing ever to happen for Music City Tonight, and she wanted to stay in touch.

Susan wanted to lie down at once, which she did when we got to her room. She said her throat was getting worse, and maybe a hot bowl of soup would help in an hour or so. She had her soup, and was sound asleep in her own bed by eight.

I was worried, went down for a beer and sandwich, then back to my own room by nine.

A Day of Sorrow and Sadness

The next morning, Susan showed no improvement. She wanted, and got, a glass of hot milk, and some soft rolls and butter and honey. We got to the airport, and Susan was allowed to board first. Again, United Airlines showed its great hospitality and care for its customers. The layover in Chicago seemed endless, but we finally got on the non-stop plane to Boise. Susan was made as comfortable as possible. An hour before landing, Susan had to be helped to the restroom by the attendant. She helped Susan back to her seat and said somberly, "Mr. Bradford, Susan was coughing blood, and is a real sick girl." There was no doctor on the plane. I asked for and received the help of the attendant and pilot, who radioed to Boise to have an ambulance waiting, and to also phone Susan's folks and said they should meet us at the airport and follow us to the hospital.

The ambulance drove right up to the plane, Susan

was lifted in gently, and she told me—almost pleading—
that I should stay with her. We got word to her folks, and
arrived at the hospital, where specialists were waiting.
Susan clung to my arm as she was wheeled into the
emergency room. The doctors took a look at her throat and
took her pulse and blood pressure and temperature. The
main specialist caught my eye, and shook his head, then
Susan was transferred to an adjacent room. Her family
followed us in, and there were two nurses there waiting to
help.

Out of Susan's hearing, the doctor said gravely,
"Susan is so weak she cannot last very long. Her system
simply has been unable to absorb all the stress. I'm so
terribly sorry to tell you that nothing can be done."

Susan was conscious, but with a smile on her face.
She whispered, "Dougie, hold my hand."

She clutched my hand tightly, and the miracle
happened. A dazzling light flashed for an instant. Susan
raised herself slightly, and exclaimed with reverence and
awe, "Oh, He is glorious!" The she quit breathing.

Eric, Gloria, and I were deeply shaken. I saw the two
nurses cross themselves. But the shining moment was
this—we all thought the same—that Jesus Himself had
come to escort Susan to Heaven.

Part of me died at the same time.

Gloria said with daze in her voice, "Susan has gone
home to the Lord," and started sobbing. Eric wrapped his
arms around her and there were tears from him, too. My
own tears started.

Outside the room, the doctor spoke tenderly, "She did
not have a chance. Her system was too far weakened, and
the huge amount of stress was too much for her. But she
had no pain." He left, shaking his head sadly.

Eric said, "Doug, we'll go home and tell Sally. We will
talk about the funeral in the morning." He seemed numb
with grief.

I caught a cab back to the airport to collect the luggage and my car, and drove blindly home. I sat in my chair all night, eating nothing and drinking nothing.

The phone calls started at six the next morning, and I got groggily up from my chair. Lorianne was first, then Charlie, Jim Owens and numerous others. All expressed deep grief and sorrow. I told them no flowers, but to contribute to their local Salvation Army people with the money earmarked for hungry children.

The morning paper had its front page dominated by "Susan Sanders, 1974–1995." The story was a glowing tribute to Susan, highlighting her career and her life. The story said nothing of the flash of light in Susan's room, and made no mention that Jesus had appeared.

It was Sunday. Gloria called and invited me to go to church with the family. Their pastor, Rev. Dunbar, had an eloquent, but simple tribute for Susan, saying she had gone to her home in Heaven.

We left the church, sad and teary, and Sally clutched my arm and was crying, "Oh Doug, why couldn't it have been me?"

"Hush, child," I replied as gently as possible. "Jesus came for Susan."

At the funeral home the next day, we gazed at Susan for the last time. She was breathtakingly beautiful. Her eyes were open and she seemed ready to speak.

The top of the casket was lowered gently, and for the last time, I saw the girl who had stolen my heart. The memory of her soft, lovely face would remain with me forever.

The cemetery was small, but immaculate. The family had requested privacy, and only a few close friends had showed up. Susan's grave was beneath a majestic evergreen. Rev. Dunbar read a few lines from the Bible, including "Let not your heart be troubled, ye believe in God, believe also in Me."

I noticed all three local TV stations had crews at the respectful distance.

Rev. Dunbar told the gathering that Mr. Bradford had a few words to say.

Until I got to my feet, I had no idea what to say. But somehow, the words started.

"Folks, we all share deep grief and sorrow, and truly it is a time of tragic sadness. But I must tell you it also must be a time for gladness. A miracle happened when Susan stopped breathing. Eric, Gloria, and I were in the room with Susan, with two nurses. A sudden, brilliant flash of light burst forth, and Susan spoke for the last time. She exclaimed, 'Oh, He's glorious!'

"Think of it. Jesus Himself had come to earth to escort Susan to Heaven. We all know that Susan was a star on earth. Now she will be a star in the Heavenly choir, in all its glory.

"I know there will be those who disbelieve, but Jesus was there, and Susan saw Him. So I say to you, even though all our hearts are heavy with sorrow, this must not be a time for sadness, but a time for gladness, because Susan is at home with the Lord. Amen."

The tears came then, and as I turned away, Eric took my hand and Gloria and Sally put their arms around me.

I noticed that only one TV crew had remained, the people from Channel 7, KTVB, the NBC network outlet in Boise.

We rode the limousine back to the funeral chapel together to our own cars, and Eric urged that I visit with them for awhile. I was numb with grief, but stopped briefly. I told them I was going home, and nobody would hear from me for a few days. Sally held my arm as she lead me to my car, and her tears were flowing and so were mine as I drove home.

<u>The Hurt is Heart Deep</u>

The next several days didn't do much to reduce the hurt. I thought about hopping in a plane, going to California, Arizona, Florida, Nashville, Knoxville, or Gatlinburg. I thought about laying in a supply of Scotch whiskey, but didn't do it. I had a supply of Heineken's on hand, and some of those low cal frozen food dinners, in case I got hungry, which wasn't very often.

I had my phone ID gimmick on, and if I didn't like who was calling, I let the answering device advise I was not available to talk.

It was several days following the funeral that the phone rang, and the machine showed New York was calling. Out of curiosity, I answered, and was asked to hold for Tom Brokaw with NBC.

Tom asked right off is my account of Jesus coming to escort Susan to Heaven was true, and I told him of course, there were five other people in the room who witnessed the flash of light.

Tom announced he was coming to Boise for personal interviews. Eric, Gloria, and I declined, but told him in private talks of what had happened, that we were entirely sure that Susan had seen Jesus Himself. Tom found the two nurses who were present, and they told the same story.

Tom told us, before leaving, that he would have a special the next week on NBC, and that he himself would declare that he was entirely convinced that Susan indeed had seen Jesus and that miracle would be featured on his special.

NBC broke this exclusive and had a record audience. But there were critics who scoffed, and the anti-Christ community tried to erase the story of Jesus in the minds of the people. The attempt failed. Pastors across the country had hundreds of sermons on the miracle, and they all endorsed the account of what had happened that fateful night.

Soon, the matter disappeared from the news.

DISNEYLAND CALLS

But excitement continued. The next week, the phone ID said Anaheim, California, was calling, so I answered, and a voice asked me to hold for Mr. Eisner.

A man's voice came on quickly, introduced himself as Michael Eisner, head of Disney Productions, and came right to the point.

"Mr. Bradford, Disney would like to do a feature movie on the life of that young woman, Susan Sanders, because those of us here at the offices admired her from the start. Would such a project be possible?"

I was stunned. Here is the president and CEO of the Disney Magic Kingdom asking to do a movie on the life of Susan.

I told him the idea was fine, but I would have to consult with Susan's parents and I would call him back if I had his phone number.

I jotted down his number and called the Sanders. Eric answered, and I asked if I could come over, that something important had developed.

They listened closely, and Eric answered for both of them.

"If the movie is clean, and a real tribute to Susan, it sounds all right," he decided. "But there must be definite stipulations—no vulgarity, no trashy sex, no violence, no hatred."

We agreed the movie rights should be generous, that neither of us wanted or needed the money, that it would be used in places where it would help a lot of people.

I called Mr. Eisner back the next morning and explained the situation, emphasizing that we must have the final approval rights of the script, a say so in casting, maybe a small percentage of the gross, sharing in the sales of any videos, plus $3 million for the rights.

He whistled, and said I was asking too much. I told him the $3 million would all go to charitable use, and that it would be tax deductible for Disney, that the other requests were flexible and would be easy to compromise.

He then suggested that the Sanders and I come to Anaheim to visit and talk business, and I explained that they both worked and could not get away. Then I made the approach.

"Mr. Eisner, I know you are one of the busiest men in the country, but would it be possible for you to jet to Boise some morning, meet the Sanders and Sally, and see some of the town, especially Boise State University?" He promised to call back in a day or two, and I so advised Eric and Gloria.

I reviewed the little I knew about this powerful, dynamic executive. He took over Disney about 1984, revitalized the Magic Kingdom and turned out one huge success after another, mostly family films. The price of Disney stock doubled and tripled, and shareholders were indeed happy.

Amazingly enough, Mr. Eisner called that his jet would arrive at the Boise airport at nine the next morning. I could meet him there, and then we could go right to the Sanders' home.

Eric and Gloria were impressed by this nice looking, forceful man who ruled the Disney empire, and Sally was, too, at being in the presence of this show business giant.

"Let's get right to business," he opened. "Mr. Bradford suggested $3 million for the movie rights to Susan's life story, and that is agreeable, since it will all be charitable contributions. We cannot pay any percentage of the gross, because all movies are too expensive to make any advance promises. We should be able to pay you $1 for each video sold after the movie has been seen. You would have complete right of final approval of the script, and it will be clean, with no vulgarity or violence or cheap sex."

The Sanders and I were quick to agree with those terms, bringing a wide smile to Mr. Eisner's face.

Mr. Eisner, acting like a fan of Susan's, commented that the Tennessee song was so pretty and catchy, and asked if there was anybody in Boise who could sing half as good as Susan.

SALLY IN THE SPOTLIGHT

Eric looked at me, and we both nodded. "Mr. Eisner, Sally is right here, she has a splendid voice and is improving every week. Sally, would you sing the song for Mr. Eisner?" I requested.

Sally gulped, and almost in a daze said she would try, so I just told her to sing the song so that Susan would be proud of her.

Sally proceeded to entrance all of us. Her voice was developing into pure and rich and sweet tones. Mr. Eisner said he was impressed, and Sally beamed.

Mr. Eisner nodded approvingly at the Boise State campus and attractive buildings. He showed great interest in Bronco Stadium, with its artificial blue turf, the only one of its kind in the country.

Then he said worriedly, "Finding the perfect girl to play Susan will be the most difficult problem." He offered that Disney might have to conduct a national search, like MGM did in the late 1930s to find a suitable Scarlett O'Hara, finally picking a British girl, Vivian Leigh for *Gone with the Wind*. He mused if Disney had a national search, it would generate massive publicity for the movie to follow.

We agreed that he would send official contracts to us within a week, which we would have our attorney inspect. Then he suggested that Mr. and Mrs. Sanders and I come to Anaheim for the official signing. "And bring Sally," he added. "She has great good looks, her voice is very, very appealing, and if we have a national search, by all means I would want Sally to enter."

As we neared the airport, I had one last question. "Mr. Eisner, why did you, as one of the busiest executives in the country, take the time to come to Boise?"

He responded carefully, "Because Susan's story is one of the sweetest and most enduring of any I have heard of. This tender story is exactly the kind that Disney likes to produce. But I expect the real reason is that I, like so many millions of other fans all of the country, loved Susan, too."

I nodded gratefully, with a lump in my throat.

Mr. Eisner's last words: "Believe me, the story of Susan, the girl with magic in her voice, will be one of our best. That you can count on. Susan deserves the best, and we will produce a movie that everybody can be proud of."

With that he climbed into his plane, which soon vanished into the southwest.

The contracts did indeed arrive within a week, our lawyer approved of them, and we made reservations to get to Anaheim, planning the trip for a day or two after Thanksgiving. I spent the holiday alone, by preference.

We met Mr. Eisner in his impressive, but not elaborate offices in Burbank, and it was as joyful as could be under the circumstances.

Mr. Eisner looked at Sally and advised her, "We plan a nationwide search for a talented, beautiful young lady to play the part of Susan. I want you to enter, and I think you would have an excellent chance of winning."

Sally started to refuse, but saw me looking at her

sternly, and she said firmly, "I am really not good enough to play Susan, but if I am lucky and get selected, I'll do the best I can."

Sally was on Cloud Nine, and I knew she would work and practice long and hard to get the part.

The Christmas season was approaching. I was lucky, but also a good planner because I had several gifts for each of the grandkids and sons and daughters-in-law and got to UPS the ones going out of town.

Sally came by with a handsome photograph of herself and Richard, by now her fiance. I had gotten her a gold necklace, not as fancy as the one I gave Susan for her birthday, but nevertheless, a valuable item. Sally was thrilled, and immediately put it on.

The holidays passed quietly. I bought a good share of AT&T with calls to Burbank and Ventura in California, Minneapolis in Minnesota, and Gooding in Idaho.

THE AGONY AND THE ECSTACY

Old man winter had been kind to Boise the first half of January 1996, but lost his temper the last half and covered Treasure Valley with coats of snow.

I woke up one noon from my beauty sleep, stiff and cramped, when the phone jangled. A surly, nasty voice demanded to speak to Josephine. I fired back just as nasty: "Josephine ain't here, Josephine don't live here. You got the wrong number," and replaced the phone with some extra force, then returned to my chair and smoked my usual after-snooze cigarette.

I decided to call Sally, to see if she had heard anything from the Disney people. I dialed 376—the prefix for a lot of West Boise phones—and drew a blank. I shook my head to chase the cobwebs, tried again, and could go no further. I cussed myself. I knew my social security number, my Mastercard and American Express card numbers, even my old Navy ID on my dog tag. I tried 376 again, but could remember no more numbers. I growled at myself for being such a dummy, and reached for the phone directory. I ran down the list of Sanders, and found no listing for Eric. I tried again.

There was no Eric Sanders listed.

I was totally confused and couldn't understand why I could not recall a number I had dialed a hundred times. Then a sudden, stabbing thought pierced and seared my mind. With agony and disbelief, I slowly realized that I had lived the most wonderful dream any man had ever had. It was the blackest moment of my life, ravaging and devastating.

I had loved a phantom beautiful young girl, a year and a half of one miracle after another unfolding, only to reluctantly realize that it had been a beautiful illusion. I checked the mantle where I had put Sally's picture. There was no picture.

I stumbled to my chair, and sank back utterly drained of emotion, but dazed and stunned. The times with Susan were so glorious and vivid and real, discovering her and being with her as she soared to stardom. There was a lump in my throat that somehow would not go away.

We had planned several trips. First to Knoxville and Pigeon Forge and Gatlinburg, because I wanted Susan to see those majestic Smoky Mountains that she sang about in her Tennessee song. Then to Burbank and Ventura in California to visit two sons and families. And also to Minneapolis to visit another son and family. We had made trips to Gooding, just a hundred miles down the pike to be with my other son and family.

I managed a weak, rueful smile, knowing I must adjust to see all the dreams shattered, crumbled, and vanished.

I moped for several days, or maybe languished is the best word. Doing some cleanup work in the back yard, I wondered if I could ever have such a magnificent dream again, and it was too bad more men didn't have the same wonderful pleasure.

Suddenly, the thought came. Miracle dreams such as mine could not die. I decided right then and there to try to write the story of that dream.

I did try, and this is it.

ONE MORE MIRACLE

But—this is not the end of the story. There's always room for one more happy miracle.

Quite often, I still thought tenderly of Susan, and one morning decided to drive by where her house should be, number 2842. Her street ended at 2840, and I smiled ruefully.

Then some power guided the car to the Performing Arts Center on the Boise State campus, where this story started about 20 months ago and where I had picked Susan up so many times.

I walked around the area, watching the young men and women entering and leaving.

Then suddenly and stunningly, a beautiful young black girl, limping slightly in her left leg, emerged from the front doors. My heart stopped beating, and I blurted, "Susan, you're real!"

This wondrously attractive young woman turned and said, "Of course I'm real, Mr. Bradford. Good to see you again, sir." With a radiant smile, she strolled towards her car.

In a deep daze, I stopped a couple of young women and asked, "Ladies, am I awake and standing outside the

Arts Center? I'm not loony, but I must ask that question." The girls looked carefully at me, and said, "Yes, Pops, you are awake and standing here with us." They seemed to want to leave at once.

I paused to take stock, and a feeling of tremendous and unbelievable happiness surged thru my heart. I *was* awake, and this time, it was no dream. Somehow the hurt and pain vanished.

There *was* a Susan, and there *is* a Susan. I rejoiced down deep inside, because another miracle had happened. I knew that Susan and I would get acquainted all over again and that there would be a future with this lovely young lady.

Don't try to unfold the secrets of miracles. They are really unexplainable, but they *do* indeed happen, and this latest miracle was the most glorious of all.

Now this story can end happily. Who knows: Maybe it is just the start of another jubilant adventure.

Written at Boise, Idaho
January, 1996